"I Want [You," He Said,]
Holding Her Tightly,
His Voice Thick.

The night was dark with clouds and the distant rumble of thunder. Raindrops from a recent shower reflected the walkway lights like crystal tears. When Holly stopped to gather the hem of her dress out of reach of the puddles, Linc lifted her into his arms with savage impatience. He walked with long strides toward the house. A fold of silk escaped her fingers, but she couldn't move to gather it up again.

"Linc—"

"No more excuses," he said in a harsh voice. "I'm not going to wait any longer."

Holly looked at his face, outlined in shadows and white light. It was the face of a stranger who knew neither kindness nor love.

"Don't look at me like that," he said impatiently. "Your game of tease and retreat is over, Shannon. Now it's my turn."

ELIZABETH LOWELL

lives in California with her journalist husband and their two children. Her beautiful marriage is responsible for her strong belief in romantic love. That belief, combined with her imaginative power and sorcery with words, makes her a favorite with romance readers.

Dear Reader:

SILHOUETTE DESIRE is an exciting new line of contemporary romances from Silhouette Books. During the past year, many Silhouette readers have written in telling us what other types of stories they'd like to read from Silhouette, and we've kept these comments and suggestions in mind in developing SILHOUETTE DESIRE.

DESIREs feature all of the elements you like to see in a romance, plus a more sensual, provocative story. So if you want to experience all the excitement, passion and joy of falling in love, then SILHOUETTE DESIRE is for you.

I hope you enjoy this book and all the wonderful stories to come from SILHOUETTE DESIRE. I'd appreciate any thoughts you'd like to share with us on new SILHOUETTE DESIRE, and I invite you to write to us at the address below:

Karen Solem
Editor-in-Chief
Silhouette Books
P.O. Box 769
New York, N.Y. 10019

ELIZABETH LOWELL
Summer Thunder

Silhouette Desire
Published by Silhouette Books New York
America's Publisher of Contemporary Romance

SILHOUETTE BOOKS, a division of Simon & Schuster, Inc.
1230 Avenue of the Americas, New York, N.Y. 10020

Distributed by Pocket Books

ISBN: 0-671-47149-X

First Silhouette Books printing July, 1983

10 9 8 7 6 5 4 3 2 1

America's Publisher of Contemporary Romance

Printed in the U.S.A.

Summer
Thunder

1

Come on, Shannon, smile like I'm your lover. You do know what a lover is, don't you, sweetie?"

The flash that burst in her face was reflected in polished metal shields held by sweating technicians. Holly Shannon North bit back what she wanted to say and smiled. Jerry was the hottest fashion photographer outside of Paris, but he had a mouth like a razor blade. Since she had refused to sleep with him, he had become impossible.

"Better, but not good. I know you're ice from the neck down, but let's keep it our secret, lovey."

Holly's smile widened. She lowered her eyelids until her sherry-colored eyes were only glints beneath thick black lashes. Long hair fell like black water over her bare shoulders. Perspiration made fine tendrils of hair curl over the high temples and slanted cheekbones that had transformed a young girl called Holly into Shannon, an internationally famous model.

"Now give me a pout. Lots of lip just begging to be

bitten. Turn left. Make that hair fly. Make every man who looks at you want to feel it sliding over his bare skin."

Holly turned with the grace that was as much a part of her as her long legs and lithe body. The heat that had everyone else short-tempered and sweating was like wine to her. She had been raised in Palm Springs' brilliant summers. The desert sun that bleached out most people made her bloom. A delicate rose flush glowed beneath her skin, hinting at the heat within, a heat that only one man had ever touched.

She tried not to think of Lincoln McKenzie, but could not help herself. The feel of Palm Springs in the summer was too unique. She could not make herself believe that she was in New York or Paris, Hong Kong or London or Rome, and Lincoln McKenzie was half a world away. She knew he lived here. He was part of the desert, as strong as the mountains rising beyond the city. Memories of him, like the sun, fired her skin.

She had worshiped Linc since she was nine years old and he was seventeen, riding one of the Arabian horses his family raised. The first time she saw him was a moment so vivid she could still smell the sage and dust, see his slow smile and hazel eyes, feel the velvet flutter of the horse's nostrils and her own heart as she stood in the path and smiled up at him.

"Lovely. Keep it up. Over the shoulder now. Turn. Faster. Again. Again. Again."

Holly turned and spun, feeling like a leaf caught in the winds of time. She did not remember when her young girl's crush on Linc had changed into something more consuming. Although their ranches shared a common boundary, the two families did not socialize. Yet she saw Linc at horse shows and auctions, and with each meeting she fell more completely under his spell. Each time, it crushed her that he did not notice her.

"Yeah, good. Now a little brighter, less pout. Big smile, baby. Gimme teeth."

Holly smiled at the camera, but her eyes were focused on the past, the night she had been baby-sitting Beth McKenzie, Linc's nine-year-old sister. The McKenzies came home very late, arguing and more than a little drunk. She had never heard people swear at one another like that. Linc showed up unexpectedly. She ran to him. He drove her home, talking softly until she stopped shaking.

When he learned that she had turned sixteen at midnight, he teased her gently about "sweet sixteen and never been kissed." What began as a comforting gesture became different, deeper, the timeless kiss of a man holding a woman he desired. She responded with an innocent abandon that had all but destroyed his control. After a long time he had taken her face between his hands and looked at her, memorizing the moment, the moonlight pouring over her.

"That's the smile!" said Jerry triumphantly. "My God, babe, if you were only half as hot as you look. Left shoulder. Gimme some heat. Yeah. Yeah! Turn on for me, babe!"

Holly barely noticed the photographer's chatter or the battery of flashes going off in her face. She was sixteen again, smiling up at the man she had always loved. Linc had wanted to take her out the following night, but she had promised to baby-sit for her father's foreman. That was where she had been when Linc came and told her there had been an accident, a head-on crash along a twisting county road.

He had driven her to the hospital where doctors were trying to save her parents. Later she discovered that his stepmother had been killed and his father critically injured; but at the time, all she knew was that Linc held her through the long night while first her mother and then her father died. He had held her while she screamed and wept, held her while her world shattered, held her until she fell into an exhausted sleep in his arms.

When she woke up, she was in a hospital bed and her mother's sister, Sandra, was there. Holly knew Sandra only from a few faded photographs in a shoe box full of family pictures.

Within a few days Sandra had taken her back to Manhattan, where she owned an agency that specialized in high-fashion models. By the time Holly was eighteen, she was working full time as a model. By the time she was nineteen, she had been on the cover of every major American and European magazine. By the time she was twenty, she was the Royce Reflection, the woman chosen by Europe's foremost designer to represent his total line of products, from perfumes to jewelry, negligees to furs.

Holly used only her middle name, Shannon, when she worked. It was her way of separating herself from the glamorous alien creature who stared back at her from the pages of magazines and spoke seductively about negligees and love on millions of television screens. Shannon was sensual, beautiful, extraordinary.

But after years of seeing herself as a rather awkward duckling, Holly was not comfortable with what makeup magicians did to her face. She came to resent the men who groped after her beauty in expensive cars and penthouse suites. She felt that the men were really making love to a four-color magazine spread. And that was how she responded—cool, sophisticated, flat. Men called her many names, frigid being the most polite. At twenty-two, she was a virgin who looked like every man's sensual dream.

"Lift your arms. Higher. Good. Now arch your back and shake out your hair. No, no, no. C'mon, sweetie, give it a little sex. Think of your lover. Oh yeah," he added in a nasty tone, "I forgot. You're not into lovers. So put your hands on those lovely, useless hips and *pretend,* damn you!"

A toss of her head sent black hair rippling down the center of Holly's back. She wished her hair had been long when Linc's fingers had tugged playfully at her chin-length curls. Why couldn't she have been beautiful then, when she was sixteen and in love? Why couldn't she be sixteen now, in Linc's arms, his mouth warm against her throat and his taste on her lips. . . .

"Beautiful!" crowed Jerry. "Babe, I'm gonna put you up for an Oscar. If I didn't know better, I'd swear you liked sex."

His words were meaningless noise to Holly. She was six years in the past, smiling, lost in her memories. She turned, hair swirling, arms held out to the only man she had ever loved. She could see him so vividly, chestnut hair shot through with gold, taller than other men, stronger. His eyes changed with the light, first hazel, then green, now dark with an emotion she could not name.

Past and present collided, throwing her off-balance. She realized that she was not holding out her arms to a dream, but to the real man. Linc was there, towering over the crouched, muttering photographer—but the look Linc was giving her was one of contempt, not love. His eyes swept the crowd of technicians and gawkers before returning to an examination of her that was so intimate she felt herself blush. She crossed her arms over her breasts and shook her hair forward until it was a veil concealing her from Linc's cold scrutiny.

"That's a new one," said Jerry, shifting for a better angle. The motor drive on his camera raced like a mechanical heart, pumping frame after frame of film through the camera. "Not bad, lovey. Now shoot out that right hip and give me the hungry little girl bit."

Holly stood frozen in Linc's contempt, her dream breaking like glass around her, cutting her.

"Wake up, Shannon," snapped Jerry.

Shannon. Not Holly. Shannon. The name echoed in her mind, reminding her that she was a professional model, not a plain, moonstruck sixteen-year-old. Automatically she assumed a provocative stance, hand on hip, chin lifted, as graceful as a lily swaying on a long stem.

"You call that a smile?" said Jerry. "Over your right shoulder. Gimme some teeth and a hint of tongue."

Holly turned. Linc had not moved. He was still there, watching her with a sardonic twist to his mouth. Suddenly she realized that the silk dress she wore was molded to her body by heat and static electricity, telling anyone with eyes that Royce designs, as the ads said, "were not made to be worn over anything but a woman's perfumed skin."

Embarrassment and something else shot through her, something she had not felt since she was sixteen. Her body changed, hot and cold at once, and her breasts showed in intimate detail against the thin silk. For an instant she was motionless, caught in Linc's consuming glance.

As she spun away, the fine silk clung to her hips. She walked through the battery of lights and reflectors without a backward look.

"Shannon?" called Jerry. "Where are you going? I'm just getting started."

"And I'm just getting finished," she said, with the brittle, East Coast accent that she used when she dealt with difficult men.

She took sunglasses and a bottle of mineral water from the catering van that followed her to every location, whether it was mountaintop, sea or desert. The van was just one of the fringe benefits of being the Royce Reflection. She put on the rose-tinted glasses and sipped at the icy water. With a sigh, she rolled the bubbly liquid around on her tongue and rubbed the bottle over the pulse that beat hotly in her wrists.

"What the hell do you think you're doing?" shouted Jerry.

She ignored him and concentrated on her hands, which showed an alarming tendency to shake. Jerry began yelling names. She ignored that, too, reminding herself that he was a great photographer as well as a miserable human being.

"Belt up, Jerry." Roger Royce's clipped British voice cut across Jerry's tirade. "You've been working Shannon like a donkey for hours. Any other model would have told you to get stuffed."

Holly turned and faced her boss. He was taller than her five feet eight inches, blond and elegantly masculine. He was a genius with shapes, textures, colors and women's bodies. He was also a gentleman.

"You okay?" asked Roger, touching her forehead with his palm. "You look pale underneath all that makeup."

"I'm fine," she said, smiling thinly. "I didn't realize he'd been at me for three hours. It caught up with me all at once."

"You're sure?" Roger turned her so that her face was not in shadow. "You *are* pale. I shouldn't have trusted Jerry. He's vicious with models who won't sleep with him."

"It's not Jerry's fault," said Holly, which was the truth. If anyone was to blame for her wan state, it was a man called Lincoln McKenzie. No, that wasn't fair. She was to blame. She was the one who had let memories and a dream seduce her. "I get wrapped up and forget about time."

"I know. It's one of the things that makes you such a fantastic model." Roger's blue eyes narrowed as he took in the lines of strain around her eyes and lips. He stroked her hair away from her face. "You look positively transparent, love. Go back to the hotel and lie out by the pool. Not too long, or—"

"—I'll get tan lines and won't be able to wear half your designs," finished Holly, smiling crookedly.

Roger laughed and gave her a quick hug. "That's why I love you. You understand me so well."

"You love every model who looks good in your clothes," she said wryly.

"Ah, but you look the best so I love you the best."

She smiled and shook her head. She took Roger seriously as a designer and as a friend, but not as a potential lover. He was wise enough to know that if he insisted on seducing her, he risked losing her, but if he settled for friendship, he would continue to have Shannon's unique presence to grace his products.

For her part, Holly felt no more physical attraction toward Roger than she had felt for any man since Linc. Roger's kindness and his quick wit, however, had made him one of her favorite people.

"Sorry to break up this little love feast," said a man's hard voice, "but I was told I'd find Roger Royce here."

Even as Holly turned, she knew she would find Linc. She could no more forget his voice than she could forget the feel of his skin beneath her palms.

"I'm Royce," said Roger.

"Lincoln McKenzie." Linc's voice was flat. He did not offer his hand or add anything to his clipped statement.

Roger looked Linc over from the top of his curly chestnut hair to the dusty soles of his cowboy boots. Like a race announcer, Roger gave a running description of what he saw. "Six four, maybe five. Good muscle development. Dreadful cowboy clothes, but you won't be wearing them if I use you. Clean hands. Good legs, lean but powerful. Expensive boots. All in all, not bad. Quite good, actually. Except for the face. Too . . . dangerous. Husbands would take one look at you and decide *not* to buy Royce products. Can you smile, Lincoln McKenzie?"

Linc's smile made a chill move down Holly's arms. She didn't know what game Roger was playing, but she knew he was playing it with the wrong man.

"No," said Roger, shaking his head. "You won't do at all. Tell your agency to send out someone pretty. And tell them to be quick about it. We shoot at Hidden Springs on Monday."

"No," said Linc.

The smile was gone, leaving only the hard planes of Linc's face. Holly couldn't help staring. This was not the Lincoln McKenzie she remembered. This man didn't look capable of tenderness. His lips were too unyielding to have the warmth and sweetness she remembered.

"No what?" said Roger. "No, your agency doesn't have anyone pretty, or no, they can't be quick about sending another male model?"

"Neither."

"Come, come," said Roger, his British accent becoming more apparent as he became more impatient. "One can carry the tight-lipped western-man act too far, you know."

Linc laughed with genuine amusement. "I'm male, but not a model. I don't have an agency, but I have seen men prettier than me. You, for instance. A nicely civilized Viking."

Roger smiled. He cocked his head to one side, reassessing the tall man in front of him. "Not a model?"

"No."

"Too bad. You have possibilities. And brains."

"I also have control of Hidden Springs."

"Oh. That's where we're going to shoot on Monday."

"No. That's where you're *not* going to shoot on Monday or any other day."

Roger frowned and released the lock of Holly's hair that he had been absently playing with. "Would you mind repeating that?"

"Not at all." Linc's smile made Holly wince, though he was not looking at her, had not looked at her since he had found her in Roger's arms. "I don't like jet-set parasites and their prostitutes. I won't have them on my ranch."

Holly was too shocked by Linc's words to defend herself or say anything about who really owned Hidden Springs. If she had been pale before, being called a prostitute made her go white.

Roger looked sideways at her. He knew that Hidden Springs was on land owned by Sandra Productions. In fact, it was Holly who had suggested that Hidden Springs would make an ideal backdrop for Roger's new line of products. He put his arm around her in a protective gesture. "I sell style, period."

Linc shrugged and looked at Holly. "You may be selling style," he said, "but she's selling something more basic."

His cool appraisal of her body was more insulting than any man's touch had ever been.

"Apologize to Shannon," said Roger, "and then leave."

"I don't apologize for telling the truth. If she can't stand the name, she should get out of the game."

Holly stepped out of the protective curve of Roger's arm and confronted Linc with a flashing, professional smile. "I'm going to enjoy the shoot at Hidden Springs," she said in a husky voice. "Knowing that you don't want us there will make every minute . . . *special.*"

"No one steps on that land without my permission."

"Really?" Holly's smile vanished. "We have a little piece of paper from the owner of that land that says we can camp there all summer if we like."

Linc's face changed, showing surprise and some other emotion that was too complex to be easily labeled. "Holly?" he said incredulously. "Do you mean that Holly North gave you permission to use Hidden Springs?"

For a moment Holly was too stunned to speak. The fact that Linc hadn't recognized her brought both relief and unexpected pain. Almost instantly she realized that she should not have been surprised that he didn't know her. The only thing about her that hadn't changed in the last six years was the unusual color of her eyes, and that was concealed behind sunglasses. Roger was also too surprised to say that Holly North and Shannon were one and the same woman. Before he could find his tongue, she spoke.

"Yes. Holly gave us permission to use Hidden Springs."

"I don't believe it," said Linc flatly. "Holly wouldn't associate with people like you."

She put a restraining hand on Roger's arm, afraid he would reveal who she was. "Let me defend Holly," she murmured. "After all, she's my very best friend." She turned to Linc again. "Do you know Holly very well?" Her voice was pure Shannon, bright and cold.

Roger snickered.

"I knew Holly." Linc's voice was as hard as the line of his mouth. "It's been six years since I saw her."

"People change," suggested Holly lightly. "They must. The Holly I know would never have put up with a dirty-minded boor."

"The Holly I knew would never hang around with prostitutes."

"On that, we are in perfect agreement," snapped Holly, dropping her brittle accent for a tone closer to outright anger.

Surprisingly, Linc smiled. "Maybe you do know her after all."

"Better than you ever did," she retorted, then regretted it. She didn't want Linc to investigate how well she knew Holly. She could not bear to know that the contempt in his eyes was directed at herself rather than the high-fashion creation called Shannon. "I know Holly well enough to guarantee that we'll shoot at Hidden Springs on Monday."

"I'm managing that land for Holly. If I say no, she'll say no."

"You'll have to get to her first," pointed out Roger, suppressing a smile. "I think she's on a desert safari."

"That's right," said Holly quickly. "She won't be back in Manhattan for weeks. I'm afraid that you lose both this battle and the whole bloody war."

"You've spoiled her," said Linc to Roger. "Mongrels need a firm hand if you want to show them in the Companion Class."

Wind whipped Holly's hair across Linc's face as she leaned forward; he flinched as though her hair were black fire. "I'll bet you're one of those tall, tight-lipped men who is good only with dogs and horses."

Roger moved uneasily. "Shannon—"

She shook off his warning and gave Linc her most seductive smile. Through the tinted glasses her eyes were dark, nearly brown, brilliant with anger and pain. To be so close to him again and see only contempt in his look was more than she could bear.

"Dogs," drawled Linc, "are docile, obedient and *loyal*, unlike beautiful women."

"You noticed," she murmured, lowering her thick lashes.

"That you're beautiful?" Linc shrugged. "Lightning's beautiful, too, but only a fool wants to touch it."

"Then crawl back under your rock, tall man," she said between her teeth. "Lightning won't reach you there."

For a moment there was only charged silence beneath the awning of the catering truck. Then a pouting, breathless voice spoke from behind Linc's back. "There you are, Linc, honey. I've been looking all over for you."

Numbly, Holly watched as the stranger rubbed against Linc's arm like a hungry cat. The woman was everything that Holly was not—tiny, blond and lushly built. Next to Linc's hard body she looked delicate and delicious. If her figure had a fault, it lay in her ample bottom; but few men would have noticed, or objected if they did.

Linc smiled down at the woman. Even though she was wearing high heels, the top of her head barely reached to his breastbone. "Hi, Cyn. Tired of shopping already?"

Cyn gave Linc a pout that Jerry would have loved to photograph. Fingernails as pink as the tip of her tongue scratched lightly down Linc's arm. "I picked out three dresses and the cutest little negligee you ever saw." When she glanced sideways at Holly, her blue eyes were as hard as glass. "It's meant for a woman, not a giraffe."

Linc laughed and wound a lock of her fine blond hair around his finger. "Sharpened your claws, too, didn't you?"

The last of Holly's dream fragmented around her as she watched the easy intimacy between the man she loved and the woman called Cyn. Holly felt like running away and hiding, but her face showed nothing at all. She was every inch the professional model posing for the most important assignment of her career. Life had taught her that you either fought or went under. She hadn't gone under when her parents died. She would survive the death of her childish dream, too.

"You bought only dresses?" murmured Holly, glancing at Cyn's hips with a knowing smile. "Roger could design a pair of pants for you. I'm sure we have some cloth around here somewhere, don't we, Roger?" Then, before he could answer, "Oh, I forgot. The material is only forty-four inches wide. That won't quite do, will it?" asked Holly with wide, innocent eyes.

Cyn's mouth sagged, then snapped shut. Her full lips flattened into a line. Before she could think of anything appropriately cutting to say, Holly dismissed her with a small smile. She turned and spoke to Linc in a voice that was both cool and oddly intimate.

"I see why you were so nasty on the subject of parasites and prostitutes," said Holly. "I'd sympathize, except you have only your own bad taste to blame." She turned her back on both of them and spoke only to Roger. "I'll be at the hotel if you need me."

With outward calm she sauntered across the burning asphalt street to her hotel. The sun was unbearably hot, scorching her body. She swallowed convulsively and prayed that no one could see the tears spilling down her cheeks.

Now, too late, she realized that she had come back to Palm Springs hoping to see Linc again, to bask in his admiration when he saw the beautiful butterfly that had come out of such a plain cocoon. Instead, she had found a taunting stranger whose contempt was a knife turning in her, cutting her to pieces.

She had been a fool to come back, and a bigger fool to believe that dreams came true.

2

Holly tossed her canteen into the back of the open Jeep, checked that the sleeping bag and ground tarp were secure, and turned to face Roger. "Quit worrying about me. I've camped at Hidden Springs since I was four years old."

"Alone?" asked Roger.

Holly ignored him. She jostled the five-gallon gas can to make sure that it was both full and secure in its bracket. Long experience with rental cars had taught her to check everything herself.

"Shannon," began Roger, then he sighed. "No, you're not Shannon now, are you?" He looked at the severely French-braided hair piled above a face innocent of makeup. Her clothes were loose, unassuming and durable. Her shoes could most kindly be described as sturdy. "You're the most amazing creature, Holly Shannon North. If it weren't for your eyes, I'd swear I don't know you. No wonder the photographers love you."

"Sure," said Holly, her tone remote. She grabbed a carton of food and cooking gear. "I'm the perfect blank canvas for men to paint their fantasies on."

Roger put his hand on her arm and squeezed gently. "I didn't mean that the way you took it."

"I know," she sighed. "I suppose I didn't mean it the way I said it, either." She lifted the carton of supplies and turned toward the Jeep.

"Let me come with you."

Holly was so surprised that she nearly dropped the carton. "You? Camping?" She smiled and shook her head. "Camping isn't your style, Roger."

"You're my style, Shan—Holly. Let me come. I promise I won't get in the way."

She stared at him. "You're serious."

"Very."

Holly felt a familiar sinking in her stomach. After yesterday, she needed to think about old dreams, broken dreams. She needed to be alone. She needed to sit in the middle of the desert silence and know that no one was going to demand anything of her, not even a smile. She needed the peace she could find in the desert.

She most certainly did *not* need to spend three days evading Roger's propositions, no matter how elegantly they were put.

"That bad?" said Roger lightly, reading her refusal in her pale lips and silence. "I just thought . . . you were so upset at what that rude cowboy said. You're all right now?"

"Yes."

"You don't sound like it." He continued like a man exploring hostile country, wary and ready to retreat instantly. "There's something between you two, isn't there?"

"No!" She dumped the carton of supplies in the back of the Jeep with unnecessary force before she turned to face Roger, giving him part of the truth, the part she could talk about without feeling like a fool. "This is the first time I've been back since my parents died. There are memories. . . ."

"I know," he said softly. "And it will be worse at Hidden Springs, won't it? You shouldn't be alone, Shannon."

As always, Roger's kindness touched her. "I'll be all right. Really." She kissed his cheek quickly. "But thanks for caring."

He caught her shoulders, holding her only inches from his lips. "I'd care more, if you'd let me."

Holly felt herself freeze up inside. She had to stop this now, before she lost one of the few people who mattered to her. "It wouldn't be worth your time," she said stiffly. "I'm frigid."

There was a moment of shocked silence. Then, "Jerry's a swine," Roger said in a ragged voice.

Holly's laugh was short and humorless. "I won't argue that. But he's right. I'm just not a sensual person."

"Rubbish! Do you think I haven't watched you? You're always touching things, tasting textures with your fingertips. Hot, cold, rough, smooth, whatever is within reach. You drink sensations. And," he added in a low voice, "your body changes when silk slides over it. You need a silken lover, Shannon, not a selfish pig like Jerry."

Memories of Linc washed over her. His body had felt exciting beneath her hands, silk over steel. She needed both the silk and the steel, the unique combination that was Linc. Silk alone, Roger alone, just wasn't enough. "I wish silk was all I needed," she whispered, surprised by the weight of tears in her lashes.

"You're crying," said Roger softly, releasing her. "I'm so sorry, Shannon. The last thing I wanted was to upset you. I just thought that maybe this time . . ." He looked at her closely. "You aren't angry, are you?"

"No," she whispered. "You?"

"It's not the first time you've said no to me," he answered with a rueful smile. The smile vanished, leaving behind an intent expression. "If you change your mind, don't be shy about telling me. Any time, Shannon. I mean that."

She nodded, but didn't look at him. "I'll meet you at the Hidden Springs gate on Monday," she said, quickly sliding behind the wheel of the Jeep. "And be sure that all the vehicles have four-wheel drive. Anything less won't make it to the springs."

The vinyl seat was brutally hot. Before she had even put the key in the ignition, her jeans felt scorched. She pulled a pair of driving gloves out of her purse, knowing that the steering wheel would be too hot to touch otherwise.

She looked up and saw Roger watching her. She grabbed a straw cowboy hat and pulled it firmly over her head. Sunglasses were next. The lenses were so dark that her eyes were invisible behind blue-green glass ovals. The Jeep surprised her by starting the first time. She shifted smoothly, backed out of the hotel parking lot and waved at Roger as she turned onto the palm-lined street.

During the white-hot days of summer, Palm Springs was a quiet place. Most of the wealthy migrated to more convivial climates. The sixty thousand people who lived in Palm Springs year round either embraced the rhythms of the desert—laze away the hottest hours and emerge at twilight—or they huddled inside air-conditioned cocoons and did not come out at all.

Holly waited at a stoplight, impatient for the signal to change and allow her to create her own breeze again. She needed the illusion of movement as much as the wind. She needed to get away. It was hotter than it had been yesterday, when Linc had appeared like a mirage and ruined her day and her dreams. Not only was it hot today, it was also humid, an unusual thing in the western desert.

The humidity was caused by moist air slowly sweeping north from the Sea of Cortez. As the hot, thick air met the mountains, it was lifted up and transformed into clouds. By the end of the day, summer thunder would peal through dry mountain canyons, shaking the land down to its granite bones. If there were enough clouds, it might even rain, cooling the incandescent country for a few sweet hours. Such cloudbursts were rare—but then, water in a desert was always rare.

Now, in the flatlands between the mountains, even the thought of coolness was impossible. Holly drove quickly, unconsciously trying to escape her uncomfortable thoughts as well as the heat. It was impossible. The memories came in waves, called up by the sound of the Jeep and the smell of metal baking beneath a summer sun.

She was pleased that childhood skills had not been lost. She had been more nervous about handling the Jeep than she had admitted to Roger or herself. She had first learned to drive her father's battered Jeep when she was a long-legged, shy fourteen-year-old begging to help feed the horses that were held in a Garner Valley pasture eight miles from the Norths' ranch. The pasture bordered on Linc's ranch. She used to go there as often as she could, hoping to see him as he rode the fence line, looking for breaks.

But she wouldn't think about that now.

After the first miles, she drove the Jeep automatically, confidently. The familiar feel of the vehicle helped to calm her as she took the Palms to Pines Highway toward the land she had not seen for six years. Sandra had turned over the management of the land to the McKenzies when Holly had refused to sell Hidden Springs.

Turning over control of the land had seemed like a good solution to Holly six years ago, for she couldn't bear to auction off the home and land that were all she had left of her childhood. And there was always the dream, hidden under layers of logic and excuses, that someday she would go back and Linc would be there, waiting for her. The gap between dreams-then and reality-now was an ache that she didn't know how to deal with.

By the time she reached the unmarked dirt road leading to Hidden Springs, clouds had condensed around the purple peaks of the San Jacinto Mountains. The air was visibly thicker, clinging to her like clouds to the mountaintops. A breeze moved restlessly across the dry land, rubbing over the brittle sage with a distant, secret sound.

The gate was locked, but the combination had not been changed since she left. Well-oiled, painfully hot to the touch even through her gloves, the lock opened with a metallic click. She took the Jeep through and locked the gate again. A tantalizing hint of coolness curled down from the mountains, riding the fitful wind. As she drove, clouds changed color and density, going from oyster to blue-tinged slate.

The road dwindled to nothing more than twin ruts winding up rocky ridges and over dry riverbeds. She watched the clouds carefully, looking for the first sign of rain in the mountain peaks rising above the road. The clouds had not yet frayed into sheets of rain. Despite that, she wasted no time when the road dipped down to cross one of the many dry washes that radiated out from the mountain slopes.

Normally the ravines held nothing more than sand and rocks and wind. A summer storm higher in the mountains could change that very quickly, even if it never rained in the lower levels. A hard rain ran off the baked land rather than soaking in. Every crack, every crevice overflowed. Rain spilled down rocky slopes in tiny streams that met and joined into walls of water that roared down formerly dry ravines.

Such flash floods usually wore themselves out in a few hours, outrunning the rainstorms that had created them. The floods left behind tangles of muddy brush, rapidly drying puddles and riverbeds that would know no water until the next storm came. To anyone who understood that mountain rains could mean desert floods, the sudden appearance of rivers in a dry land was more exciting than dangerous.

Even so, Holly breathed a silent sigh of relief as the Jeep churned up out of Antelope Wash, the last big ravine between her and Hidden Springs. She was well above the desert floor now, into the chaparral zone. A few thousand feet higher would bring her to the first pines. The road did not go that far into the mountains, however. The twisting, rock-strewn ruts ended less than a mile away, where water welled silently from the base of a shattered cliff.

Thunder rolled across the peaks, pursuing fickle lightning, never quite catching up. Clouds veiled the mountains, bathing granite peaks in mist. Though the wind was stronger now, cooler, there was still no smell of rain. For all their tossing and flirting, the clouds weren't yet ready to embrace the land.

Holly unloaded her gear and then drove the Jeep a hundred yards from the place she had chosen for her camp. If lightning danced over the land, she didn't want to be sleeping near the only metal on the mountainside. Nor did she pitch her tent too close to the five rocky pools that glittered like gemstones along the cliff's base. As much as she liked water, she liked the desert animals better. Bighorn sheep drank at the springs. If she crowded too close to the water, the animals would stay among the dry rocks, waiting and thirsting until the thoughtless intruder left.

Thunder rumbled down the granite face of Hidden Springs as Holly finished making a trench around her tent to carry off any rain that might come. She stood up and measured the sky. The sun was no more than a pale disc burning behind clouds that thickened and changed as she watched. Streamers of mist flowed down the flanks of stone peaks, softening their masculine angles. Lightning flickered too fast to be clearly seen in the late-afternoon light. Thunder came again, closer now, carried on a rising wind.

The air was more intoxicating to Holly than any wine. She laughed aloud and stretched her arms as though to hold both clouds and mountains. She knew that later, when she was cold and wet and water overflowed her careful trench, she would rue the moment she had greeted the storm with laughter and open arms. Yet at this instant she was like the land, hot and dry, waiting for the pouring moment of release.

Sunset was as sudden as thunder. Light drained out of the sky between one moment and the next. Needles of lightning stitched randomly through the clouds. She smelled rain, but none came down. She knew that somewhere above her on the mountainside clouds were pouring themselves into the land. Somewhere water was brawling down dry ravines, playfully juggling boulders as big as her Jeep. Somewhere the waiting had ended and the storm had begun. But not here, not yet. Here there was only her and the silence between bouts of thunder.

Even when she lay within the tent trying to fall asleep, the rain had not yet come. It was cooler, though, almost cold. Lightning flared randomly over the rocky land, pulling thunder behind like another color of darkness. Then came a different noise, hoofbeats pounding down the mountainside. She couldn't tell the exact direction the horse was coming from, for the rocky cliffs and ravines baffled hoofbeats, adding echos that overlapped and faded and changed directions until she wondered if she had imagined the sounds in the first place.

White light shattered over the tent, followed instantly by an explosion of noise so great she did not identify it as thunder. Blinding light and black sound alternated with dazzling speed. Wild hoofbeats rattled in the silence between thunderclaps. Somewhere near her camp a horse was fleeing mindlessly, terrified by the storm.

Holly came out of her tent at a run. She knew she had little chance of helping the panicked animal, but she wasn't able simply to cower in her tent and listen to the horse's mindless scream. She ran to the shelter of a boulder field just up the slope from her tent. Crouched with her back to the wind, she stared into the night.

There was an explosion of sheet lightning that lit up the sky from horizon to horizon, freezing time into a black-and-silver portrait of a horse rearing wildly on the low ridge just above her camp. Nearly lost in the horse's long flying mane, a rider fought to control his crazed mount. For an instant it seemed the rider would win. Then thunder came again, breaking apart the world. Black sound and white sky melded into light so fierce that the eye could not see, sound so brutal that the ear heard only silence.

Lightning came in an incandescent barrage, outlining the plunging horse. Holly knew the ridge, knew it was impossible for a running horse to keep its feet. With each new stroke of white light, she expected to see the horse go down, smashing itself and its rider against granite boulders.

She didn't know at what moment she realized that the rider was Linc. She only knew that she was calling his name, screaming at him to jump, even though she knew he could not possibly hear her. She couldn't even hear herself, though her throat was tearing apart with the force of her cries. Yet she kept on screaming at him to jump because that was the only way he could save himself from the mindless terror that drove his horse.

She made an anguished sound when she realized that Linc had no intention of abandoning the horse. He was deep in the saddle, using all his strength and skill to keep the horse from going down, riding a whirlwind with a savage determination to save both of them.

Holly didn't blame Linc for wanting to save the horse from its own folly. Even in the grip of panic, the Arabian was magnificent. Its body rippled with muscular beauty. It moved with a cat's quickness and grace. Linc, too, was magnificent to watch, so extraordinary in his skill and strength that she forgot to be afraid for him. He was part of the horse, shifting his weight from instant to instant, braced in the stirrups, using his powerful shoulders to drag up the horse's head whenever the animal stumbled.

She began to believe that horse and rider would survive the treacherous ridge. Then the world turned inside out and an ocean poured out of the sky. Instantly, she was up and running toward the ridge. She knew that no skill, no strength, nothing but a miracle could prevent the Arabian from going down in the greasy mud created during the first instants of the cloudburst.

The inevitable fall came during a burst of lightning, the horse twisting and turning, trying to keep its feet where nothing could walk much less run. At the last possible instant Linc kicked free of the somersaulting animal. He fell like the trained horseman he was, head tucked in, body relaxed, ready to roll and absorb the worst of the impact. He did everything possible, but there was nothing he could do about the boulders in his path.

Holly ran through the rain, crying soundlessly. The ground turned to grease beneath her feet, sending her staggering and sliding. A river of rain poured over her, choking her.

She found the horse first. It was lying on its side, trembling all over, drenched with rain and lather. As she watched, the animal groaned and heaved itself to its feet. It took a few tentative steps, then stood docilely, not even flinching when lightning sizzled across the ridge. For the moment, the Arabian was too stunned by its fall to be afraid of anything.

Holly clawed up the last few feet to the boulder that

had so brutally stopped Linc's fall. Lightning forked across the sky, revealing Linc. He lay on his back, motionless. She skidded to her knees beside him, shaking with fear.

"Linc!"

Her voice was hoarse, no match for the thunder boiling through the night. She crouched over him, sheltering his face from the downpour. Bursts of lightning outlined him harshly. A cut beneath his hair bled; the blood looked black in the white light. His shirt was shredded down his right side, but beneath the ribbons of cloth his chest rose and fell in even rhythms.

For a moment Holly was too dizzy with relief to do anything but put her hand on his chest and feel the strong beat of his heart. Alive, yes, but not yet safe. If he was injured, she wasn't strong enough to carry him to the tent. Yet she had to get him out of the chilling rain.

Lightning came again, followed slowly by thunder. The center of the storm was moving away. Rain still fell hard and steady, but it no longer qualified as a cloudburst. The first, most violent minutes of the storm were over.

Gently, very carefully, Holly ran her hands over Linc's arms and legs, searching for obvious injuries. She felt nothing but the resilience of his muscles beneath his soaked clothes. She moved her fingertips lightly over his chest, searching for any swelling that might tell of cracked or broken ribs.

He groaned, startling her. She snatched back her hand before she realized that her light touch hadn't hurt him. As he struggled out of unconsciousness, his head moved slowly from side to side, easing the fear she had been afraid even to acknowledge; his neck was not broken. Suddenly he rolled onto his side and tried to sit up. He grabbed his head and groaned again.

"Linc?"

As he turned toward the sound, lightning burst. His eyes were dark, dazed. "What—?"

"Your horse fell," said Holly loudly, trying to make him understand between bouts of thunder. "Your—horse—fell."

He started to nod in acknowledgment, then grimaced and held his head again. When his right hand dropped, it was streaked with blood.

"Can you stand?" she shouted, staring anxiously into the darkness that divided violent bursts of lightning. The worst of the storm might be abating, but it was far from over.

With her help, Linc pulled himself into a sitting position. She touched the right side of his head with gentle fingertips and found a small swelling at the base of his skull where blood seeped. She had no way of knowing whether he had a concussion or simply a cut.

"Do you hurt anywhere else?" she asked. She had to repeat the question several times before Linc's head moved in a slow negative gesture.

"Stand up," she said urgently. "I'll help you, but I can't carry you. Please, Linc. Stand up!"

Using the boulder and Holly, Linc managed to lever himself to his feet. She supported him anxiously while dizziness nearly overwhelmed him. After a few false starts, she adjusted to his uneven stride. Together, they reeled and staggered down the slope toward the tent.

A small battery-powered lamp filled the tent's interior with yellow light. And, for the moment at least, everything was dry. As she eased Linc onto the floor, she realized that he was shivering uncontrollably. She had to get him warm, quickly. She tore off what was left of his shirt. His soaked boots and jeans were harder to remove. As she struggled to drag the jeans down his legs, she was divided between frustration at the stubborn material and admiration for the powerful lines of his body.

The sleeping bag she had rented was large, loose and light. It would not radiate back body heat very efficiently, but it was all she had. She unzipped the slippery nylon bag with three quick strokes, rolled Linc inside and zipped the bag shut again.

His eyes opened. When he realized that he was inside a tent, he started to sit up.

"No," said Holly, holding him down with her hands on his shoulders. "You have to get warm."

"Horse." His voice was barely a whisper. "My horse."

"It was on its feet before you were."

Lightning bleached the interior of the tent. Thunder came like a falling mountain. Linc sat up, sweeping aside her hands with a strength that frightened her. Even dazed and injured, he was far stronger than she was. Dizziness struck him again, chaining him for a moment.

"I'll take care of your horse," she said hurriedly, knowing that he was too stunned to realize his own danger and not rational enough to argue with. "Stay here. Do you understand?"

With an effort, Linc nodded. She helped him lie down again, grabbed a pocket flashlight and went back out into the storm.

For the first time she really noticed the rain. The drops were almost icy, for they had condensed at high altitudes. She shivered repeatedly as she worked over the horse. Its body heat steamed outward, draining warmth into the chill air. She led the horse down to the partial shelter of boulders and chaparral.

A barrage of lightning made the animal shy violently, jerking Holly off her feet. She scrambled upright again, tore off her blouse and blindfolded the animal. It stood absolutely still, ignoring lightning and thunder alike. She loosened the cinch and rummaged in the saddlebags, hoping to find a hobble. There was only a ball of rough twine. At the first yank, twine would either give way or cut the horse's legs to the bone.

She took a deep breath, peeled off the blindfold and quickly twisted it into a semblance of a hobble. As she bound the horse's front legs, it sniffed her wet hair, snorted wearily and gave up all thought of fear and flight. It did not even object when she threw a flapping ground tarp over its back and laced everything in place with twine.

By the time Holly got inside the tent, she was shaking so hard it was almost impossible for her to get out of her wet clothes. She dug out dry jeans and a jacket, yanked them on and crawled over to check Linc. He was neither awake nor quite asleep. His skin was cold. She knew just enough about hypothermia and shock to be afraid for him. Yet there was nothing more she could do. Even if she could get him to the Jeep, Antelope Wash would be impassable.

She looked at the dark hair curling down over his forehead, framing the strong face that had haunted her dreams. His eyebrows were thick dark arches spiked with gold. His mouth, usually generous with laughter, was drawn with cold and pain. Drops of water gleamed in his moustache. How many times she had dreamed of seeing him again, touching him and feeling his touch, hearing his laughter and tasting him on her lips. What had changed him from the gentle, passionate man of her memories? Why had he become cruel and sarcastic, cold eyes watching her, words cutting her until she bled.

Slowly she bent to brush her lips over his. For a long moment she kissed him, warming his cool lips, tasting the raindrops beaded in his moustache, trembling with memories. She was ashamed of stealing back a piece of her dream while he slept, unable to protest. Yet she couldn't help herself; nor did she want to. It was little enough to warm the emptiness in her.

When she lifted her head, there were tears caught in her lashes. She watched Linc for long moments, reassured by his strong heartbeat and the easy rise and fall of his chest. She began to dread the coming morning, when he would wake up, realize she was Shannon and stare at her with cold-eyed contempt. But there was nothing she could do about that. Tonight they needed each other on the most primitive level—sheer animal warmth.

She unzipped the bag and crawled in. There was barely room to breathe, for the sleeping bag had not been designed to hold two people, especially when one of them was the size of Linc. Shaking with cold, she switched off the lamp and zipped up the bag once more. After a long time, their shared warmth heated the bag enough for both of them to sink into troubled sleep.

She dreamed that she woke up in Linc's arms, his lips against her neck, her body pressed along his. The tip of his tongue teased her lips until she sighed and smiled, giving herself to his kiss with the sensual abandon that only he had ever drawn out of her. She felt his breath against her ear and shivered with delight. His hand slid over her thin jacket, caressing her breast. His touch was more vivid than any dream of him she had ever had before.

Her eyes flew open. Daylight glowed in the tent, but not half so warmly as Linc's eyes.

"Holly," he murmured, tracing her lips with his tongue. "My sweet Holly. I thought I had only dreamed you."

3

You recognize me," said Holly, suddenly nervous.

He smiled. "It would take more than a rap on the head to make me forget you, Holly."

"But yesterday—"

"All I remember about last night is that it was dark and a mountain fell on me." His tongue slid between her lips, moved slowly. "Now if you had kissed me before you dragged me into your bed, I'd have known you no matter how dark it was." His voice changed, husky and intimate. "You taste the same as you did six years ago, sweet as a desert spring."

She drew a shaky breath, remembering the stolen kiss last night and the kisses before, six long years before. She looked at his eyes, at his face. Nowhere did she see the harsh contempt that had been there yesterday. She reached up and kissed him with trembling lips. "You taste the same, too."

"Water?" he asked whimsically, lifting his head and smiling down at her.

"Half right," she teased.

"What's the other half?"

"Fire."

Linc's arms tightened until she couldn't breathe. She had forgotten how strong he was, enough strength to make or break a world. Her world.

"Firewater," he said, laughing against her neck, sending shivers of delight over her skin. "From an illegal still, no doubt?"

She nodded her head solemnly, like a small child. "It's way up in the mountains."

"What goes into the still—cactus and pinecones?"

"No," she said, smiling and tickling her lips against his moustache. "Lightning, sage and rain." The laughter faded from her voice. "I've tasted you in my dreams, Linc."

His breath drew in sharply. His tongue probed the hollow of her throat, then moved slowly up her neck until he found her ear. His teeth closed delicately on her earlobe. When the tip of his tongue traced the curves of her ear, she began to tremble. With half-closed eyes, she rubbed her palms over his back. His skin stretched smoothly over muscles hardened by work. Silk and steel, the taste of Linc on her lips, dream come true.

"Which is better—this or dreams?" he asked softly.

"This," she murmured, moving against him, savoring his skin with her fingertips and lips. "This is better than any dream." She felt a tremor go through him and remembered how chilled he had been last night. "Are you cold?"

"Hardly," he said. He nibbled on her lips when she would have spoken her doubts. Laughter curled in his voice. "If you don't believe me, run your hands down my front instead of my back."

Abruptly, Holly remembered that Linc was naked. She jerked her hands off his skin. "I forgot I'd undressed you—but you were wet and—I'm sorry," she said helplessly.

"I'm not," he murmured, rubbing his lips over her

mouth. "In fact"—his hand slid up to her jacket zipper—"I'm going to return the favor."

"But I'm not wearing a blouse!" she said frantically.

His only answer was a ragged breath as the zipper slid down to her waist and the jacket fell open. She was so shocked she couldn't say a word. His dark head bent. The tongue that had teased her lips stroked slowly over her breast. As he blew gently across her, she felt her breast swell and her nipple harden. She made a low sound, gripped by feelings she had neither the experience nor the words to describe.

By the time his mouth melted over her other breast, she was no longer shocked. She shivered again and again, her fingers kneading his back. Her body did not feel like it was her own. Sensations raced through her, fine wires tightening with each caress, each hot movement of his tongue, tightening until she felt like twisting and moaning.

"I want to see you," he said, his voice another kind of caress.

He reached across her, unzipped the sleeping bag halfway down and pushed it away. No bathing suit lines marred the smooth flow of her golden skin, the swell of breasts taut with desire, nipples the same dusky rose as her lips.

A slow flush bloomed beneath her tan as she realized that she was lying half-naked while Linc looked at her, his hazel eyes smoky with desire. She pulled her hands away from his back and tried to zip up her jacket. He laced his fingers through hers, holding her hands in a gentle vise.

"If I had undressed you six years ago," he whispered, "I never would have let Sandra take you away."

His head lowered again, and again she felt his tongue set fire to her skin. She arched against him, wanting only to be closer, to feel more of his body covering her, to bury her fingers in his hair and hold his mouth against her forever. As though he knew what she wanted, he released her hands. Her fingers raked up his back, then burrowed into his hair. In the instant before he flinched, she remembered his injury.

"I'm sorry," she said breathlessly. "Does it hurt?"

"Only when you stop touching me."

She looked at his eyes and felt her breath stop. Even in her dreams he had not wanted her so much. Very gently she turned his head so that she could see the swelling just beneath his ear. Her breath hissed out. The bruise was darker than it had been last night. Its center was a crust of blood. "You must have a terrible headache."

He smiled crookedly. "That's the woman's line."

She laughed. "I've got some aspirin in my kit."

"There are other kinds of aches."

His hands closed over her arms, holding her when she would have left the sleeping bag.

"Take two aspirin—" she began.

"—and call you in the morning," he finished, covering his face with a groan. "That's nearly as old as the line about headaches."

"Serves you right," she said impishly, slipping out of the bag before he could stop her.

When she tried to close her jacket, the zipper jammed at the bottom. She fussed with it for a moment, then gave up. She overlapped the front and stuffed the jacket into her pants like a blouse. Then she addressed the problem of finding a small first-aid kit in a large duffel bag. She dragged the duffel onto her lap and forced her arm into the open end, trying to find the kit by a combination of memory and touch.

As she worked, her jacket slowly pulled open, revealing and then concealing her breasts in a display that was as unintentional as it was erotic. Linc watched with half-closed eyes. She made an exasperated sound and shook the bag, her breasts swaying in echo of her movements. He groaned and looked away.

Holly's head snapped up. A worried expression pinched her face. "Lie down, Linc. Please."

Her fingers felt a smooth plastic bottle. She yanked it out, shook two aspirin into her hand, hesitated, then added two more. She grabbed the canteen out from under a pile of Linc's soggy clothing and went back to him.

"Here." She knelt in front of him, holding out the pills in one hand and the canteen in the other.

"Four?" he said.

"I usually take two and you're twice as big as I am."

His eyes moved from her unique slanted eyes to the well-shaped nails on her bare feet. His hand curled around her foot and his thumb caressed her arch. "How about if I take you twice and to hell with calling the doctor. . . ."

A tremor of desire moved over her. Mutely, she held out the aspirin and water. He leaned forward, but not to take the aspirin. He eased the jacket off her shoulders until it settled around her elbows, softly binding her arms to her sides. Slowly, deliberately, he caressed her with tongue and teeth until she forgot to breathe.

Her eyes glowed nearly gold as she looked down at the dark head bent over her breasts. She saw his tongue touch her, saw herself respond, saw him look up at her. She knew her feelings must be as naked as his tongue and she didn't care. Since she was eighteen, men had been telling her how gorgeous she was. This was the first time she believed it, and Linc hadn't said a word.

"You make me feel so beautiful," she whispered.

He made a sound that could have been her name, then kissed her with a fierce possession that she met and matched. He rolled onto his back, pulling her with him until she lay half across him. His hands kneaded down her back to her hips, silently demanding another kind of caress. She molded to him, stretching against his hard body, feeling weak and strong at the same time.

The repeated neighing of Linc's horse finally penetrated their sensual daze. The animal's disconsolate sounds told them it was working itself into a frenzy. Reluctantly, Holly shifted her weight and began a slow slide off Linc's body.

"Hold still," he said. He pressed her face between his hands and fought to control his breathing. After a few moments, he succeeded. "Holly North," he sighed, "you are the only thing on God's earth that could make me forget to take care of my horse. You're dangerous, woman."

"Me?" Holly sat up slowly. She tried to laugh, but her breath kept catching in her throat. "If I'm dangerous, you're outright lethal."

He admired the flush spreading up from her breasts and her eyes brilliant with desire. He leaned toward her. "Let's argue about it," he suggested, teasing her with his tongue. "Two falls out of three?"

The horse neighed again, a shrill, frightened sound.

"Damn!" groaned Linc.

"I'll check him while you take your aspirin."

"What aspirin?" he asked innocently.

A startled look came over her face. She held her hands open in front of her, palms up. No aspirin. She looked at the rumpled sleeping bag that covered Linc like an oversized pair of pants. She spotted one aspirin quickly, caught in the same fold as the canteen. The second and third weren't hard to find, but the fourth eluded her.

Linc washed down three powdery pills with water from the canteen. "Maybe the last aspirin is inside the sleeping bag."

"You look for it, then," she retorted.

"It would be more fun if you did. Who knows what you'd find?"

Holly felt the heat of a blush and something more spread over her skin, yet she couldn't help laughing at Linc's outrageous teasing. "I found the other pills at the top of the bag, not the bottom."

"I was hoping you hadn't noticed." He laughed suddenly. "Bet I can find the fourth aspirin before you do."

Holly turned to look behind her, assuming that he had spotted the pill on the tent floor. She felt his fingertips brush beneath her breast. Startled, she looked back. In his hand was a white pill that looked a bit wilted around the edges. She realized that it must have been beneath her breast, held to her body by the fine mist of desire that suffused her.

"An aspirin after my own heart," he said, his voice rich with laughter.

She shook her head in helpless embarrassment. "I'll get you another one."

His hand closed gently on her thigh, holding her in place. "No," he said softly. "I want this one."

His eyes held hers as he put the aspirin on his tongue. When the pill vanished behind his lips, it was as though he had taken part of her into himself. He leaned forward, nuzzling under her breast, his tongue licking up the last of the fine powder that clung to her skin. His hand slid between her thighs, rubbing upward until he cupped around her. His palm moved in slow circular motions, savoring the special heat of her desire.

The wires of sensation that had been tightening in her exploded into a network of fire that raced from the pit of her stomach throughout her body. Her fingers dug convulsively into the hard muscles of his arms. "Linc," she moaned, "what are you doing?"

"Taking my medicine," he said, gently biting the taut flesh of her stomach.

The horse neighed, a high, wild sound.

"Linc—"

"Yes, I hear him," he said, his tongue moving across her navel, lingering, probing. He lifted his head with a groan as the horse's cry ascended into a scream. "Why did I have to raise horses? Why couldn't I have chosen something nice and quiet?" he asked, his voice thick with passion and exasperation.

"Like plants?" suggested Holly, laughing raggedly.

"Like rocks." His hand slid from between her legs so slowly that she moaned again. "Don't," he whispered hoarsely. "When you do that I want to take off all your clothes, to taste every bit of you until you scream." Suddenly he buried his face in her warmth.

The intimacy of his caress surprised her, holding her motionless for an instant. He sensed the change and swore pungently.

"You're right," he said, releasing her. "Sand Dancer sounds like he's either in trouble or planning to get that way."

She was empty when he didn't touch her. She wanted nothing more than to feel him pressed against her again, to hold him until the burning in her body consumed them both. She felt his eyes watching her and knew that her thoughts were as plain to him as if she had spoken them aloud.

She eased her hands out of his hair, feeling each crisp lock sliding between her sensitive fingers. With hands that shook so much she was clumsy, she tucked in her jacket once more. He didn't offer to help. She didn't ask. Both knew that if he touched her again, he wouldn't let her go.

She jammed her feet into her shoes and untied the tent flap, letting in a bright triangle of light. She turned back to Linc, then forgot what she had been going to say.

He was reaching for his clothes. Sunlight poured over his skin, turning it into polished bronze. Muscles coiled and shifted smoothly, powerfully, telling of a strength he accepted as casually as he accepted the number of fingers on his hands. The dark hairs on his body burned like molten amber, shimmering and shifting with each move he made.

Then he turned onto his side and the sleeping bag fell off his hips. She thought distantly that she should be embarrassed or appalled, but she was neither. His male beauty transcended narrow definitions of right and wrong, wise and foolish, proper and improper.

She looked away finally, only to find herself caught and held by his eyes. She knew he had been watching her even as she watched him. She remembered how it had felt to be nearly naked in his arms, his breath hot against her body, his mouth separated from her by a single thickness of cloth.

"Come here, Holly." His voice was husky, urgent.

As though at a distance, she heard the Arabian's frantic neighing. With a harsh, frustrated sound, she left the tent.

After the intimate twilight of the tent, the sun was blinding. Though the damp ground sent tendrils of vapor into the air, there were few puddles left. Once softened, the land drank water like a tawny sponge. As she pushed her way through clumps of brush, branches shaken by her passage drenched her with water and the pungent smell of sage.

The Arabian stood with his head up, ears pricked forward until the tips almost touched. The tarp she had tied onto him had slipped to one side, but her blouse had been an effective hobble. The horse snorted, watching her with dark, wary eyes.

Holly spoke in low, reassuring tones. "Good morning, Sand Dancer. You look like a mess, what with your grubby white hobble and your pea-soup tarp. The twine doesn't do much for the ensemble, either."

Sand Dancer snorted and stretched his nose toward her.

She stood quietly while the horse whuffed over her, drinking her scent. Then the velvet nose bumped her gently, accepting her as a friend. She rubbed the horse's ears, admiring their expressive elegance. Dancer's nose bumped her again, less gently.

"Friendly beast, aren't you?" she said, laughing.

"Like his owner," said Linc.

She turned and saw him standing just out of reach. He wore no shirt because it had been shredded in his fall. His jeans were still wet. They fitted his body the way she wanted to, an unbroken line of intimacy.

"Dancer's all right. Are you?" she asked, knowing she sounded breathless and unable to do much about it.

His right eyebrow lifted. "Cold wet shower, cold wet jeans—either one gets the job done. For a time."

"I meant—" She felt herself blushing and groaned. "Good Lord, you have me acting like I'm nine again."

"You must have been a very advanced nine," he teased. Then he relented. "My head aches, my shoulder is stiff and my knee is tender." He smiled. "Don't look so stricken, Holly. I've been hurt worse tripping over my own feet."

"Somehow I can't see you being clumsy," she said, shaking her head. "I've been jealous of the way you move since the first time I saw you. That and your eyelashes. Do you have any idea, Lincoln McKenzie, just how devastating your coordination and thick lashes were to this nine-year-old? And you never even noticed me for *seven years*."

"Don't bet on it. The thoughts that crossed my mind after you were fourteen would have gotten me arrested."

She stared at him for a long moment, realizing that he wasn't joking. "I wish you'd told me."

"Great," he said wryly. "Then you could have visited me in jail on alternate Thursdays."

Dancer bumped her with his nose, claiming her attention. She turned around. Linc walked up behind her and stood so close she could feel the heat of his body radiating through the back of her jacket.

"My hands are cold," he lied, rubbing his palms over her arms and then cupping her breasts until the nipples hardened between his fingers. With a soft curse he put his hands behind his back. "I'm not to be trusted this morning."

"Put your hands in your pockets," suggested Holly lightly, working over the knotted twine on the tarp with fingers that refused to stop trembling.

"They won't fit in my pockets," he admitted. His hands eased into the front pockets of her jeans. "Can I use yours?" Inside her pockets, his hands moved in sensual rhythms.

"Linc," she said raggedly, feeling herself melt with each touch, "Linc . . ."

He shuddered and pulled his hands out of her pockets. "The things you do to my self-control, woman. I thought I was long past the age when I couldn't keep my hands to myself."

"I wasn't complaining," she said softly, turning to him.

"I know. We'll make a deal, though. I won't touch you until poor Sand Dancer is taken care of. Shake on it?" he offered, holding out his hand. At the same moment they both realized that he was waiting to feel the warmth of her hand sliding across his palm. He dropped his hand. "I'll take your word for it."

Together they attacked the twine knots holding the tarp on the horse. After a night of being soaked by rain and pulled by the horse's restless movements, the knots were as hard as wood.

"Are you getting anywhere?" she asked after a moment.

"Nope."

Automatically, Holly reached into her pocket for the jackknife she always carried when she was in the desert, then remembered that her knife was in her wet jeans. She thought of the saddlebags, reached underneath the tarp—and found Linc's hand. Startled, she looked over the horse's back.

Linc was watching her, smiling. His fingernails curled across her sensitive palm as his hand withdrew. He opened the knife and went to work on the stubborn twine. Suddenly he stopped. "I don't remember fixing up this tarp for Dancer."

"You didn't," said Holly, pulling twine out of the tarp's metal-ringed eyelets as soon as the knots were cut.

"You did?"

Holly laughed. "Can't you tell? No matter how many times you scolded me, I still tie grannies in a pinch."

"In a pinch, getting the job done is all that counts."

He cut away the last of the twine and peeled off the tarp. The bridle was neatly tied to the saddle horn and the cinch had been loosened enough for the horse's comfort but not enough to let the saddle slide or turn. He glanced around, measuring the shelter provided by the tall boulders and chaparral. Then the muddy hobble caught his eye. He knelt and fingered the cloth. Like the cinch, the hobble was neither too tight nor too loose.

"Dancer's all right, isn't he?" Holly asked.

"Dancer's better than he deserves, after his performance last night." Linc stood up with casual grace. "He was just yelling because he was alone." He looked at her closely. "What happened last night? I don't remember much after Dancer went down."

"I saw you up on the ridge. Dancer was crazy with fear. You should have jumped, Linc," she said tightly. "I screamed and screamed for you to jump, but you didn't hear me. Then it began to pour. Dancer went down. You threw yourself clear." She bit her lip, remembering. "You rolled twice and then the boulder . . ." Her fingers touched his mouth as though to feel his breath and reassure herself that he was alive.

"When I reached you, your face was turned up to that awful rain and you weren't moving. I thought you were dead." She tried to smile. "I was glad to hear you groan. After a while we got you on your feet and staggered to the tent." This time her smile succeeded. "I wish I had a movie of that—thunder and lightning and rain like the end of the world, and the two of us slip-sliding down the ridge. I felt like a tugboat with a runaway ocean liner."

"We're lucky we didn't get cooked by lightning," said Linc, remembering the shattering bolts that had sent Sand Dancer into a frenzy. "What happened after we got to the tent?"

"I took off your wet clothes and stuffed you into the sleeping bag. Suddenly you wanted to go and take care of Dancer. You weren't in any shape for it, so—" She shrugged and waved her hand at the scraps of twine. "Granny knots."

"You should have waited until the storm let up."

"You're a lot stronger than I am, even when you're half dead from cold and getting rapped on the skull by a boulder," she said in a dry voice. "You didn't want to wait."

"You mean I sent you back out into that storm?" said Linc, his voice tight.

"It was you or me, and I was in better shape at the time."

"My God, Holly." He pulled her roughly against him. "You should have let me go. You could have been hurt."

"You already were hurt," she pointed out.

"Still—"

"Linc," she said, exasperated, "what kind of person do you think I am? You were *hurt.*"

"And you were alone in a wild storm with a horse that went crazy every time the sky lit up."

"I blindfolded him," she said simply.

His hands framed her face as he studied her deceptively fragile face. His thumbs stroked her cheekbones. "You're incredible," he whispered. "Clever and long legged and wild, with eyes like gold coins . . ."

Suddenly she was acutely conscious of the sunlight glinting in his hair and moustache and eyes, the tempting line of his lips, his tongue so quick and moist.

A muscle moved and tightened along Linc's jaw as he controlled his impulse to kiss her until they were both breathless. Very carefully he let go of her and turned his attention to Dancer's hobble. "Where did you get this?" he asked as he worked over the knot. "I don't remember having a spare shirt in the saddlebag."

"It's my blouse. That's why I wasn't wearing anything under my jacket when you—"

Abruptly, she stopped. The thought of the moment Linc had unzipped her jacket made her quiver deep inside her body.

"Holly," he said wonderingly, "it's a miracle I can keep my hands off you from one minute to the next. But I'm trying. God knows I'm trying."

He removed the hobble and untwisted the fabric of her blouse. The material was stained. Fine sorrel hairs stuck to it in random patches. He held up the blouse and shook his head. "I'd stick with the jacket if I were you."

"I've got another blouse."

"Too bad," he sighed. "I like the way the jacket fastens." His eyes lit with silent laughter as he untied the bridle and slipped it over Dancer's head. "Come on, boy, let's see how thirsty you are."

They both watched the horse move until they were sure that the animal suffered from nothing more serious than a few stiff muscles. Then Linc nodded, smiled approvingly at Holly and took her hand.

"Seems like old times," he said. "The springs, the smell of sage, a horse and"—he gave her a teasing sideways look—"a rumpled munchkin watching me with gold eyes."

Suddenly his glance changed, probing her face as a new thought came to him. "Why are you here, Holly? And why didn't you call and tell me you were back in California?"

4

For an instant Holly froze. She had forgotten that she was the Royce Reflection rather than the innocent sixteen-year-old of her memories . . . and his. She walked the short distance to the springs in silence, feeling his watchful eyes on her face. She didn't want to tell him that she was Shannon, but she couldn't bring herself to lie.

"I didn't call because I didn't know if you'd want to see me. You never wrote to me, not even a Christmas card," she said, remembering her disappointment when her own cards had gone unanswered.

"I wrote three times," he said. "The third time I got back a note from Sandra. She told me that my letters upset you. I gave up then. I assumed Sandra had taught you to hate me."

"Hate you? Why would I hate you?"

Without answering, he looped the reins around Dancer's neck and let the horse wander the remaining distance to the first of the pools. When he turned back to her again, his face was impassive. "My father was driving the car that killed your parents." His voice was as blunt as his words. He was utterly still, watching her response. When he saw no revulsion, he let out his breath. "You knew."

"Sandra told me. But what does that have to do with hating you? It was an accident, Linc. A rainy night and a rotten mountain road and a car that went out of control." Her lips trembled for a moment. "And your stepmother died, too. An accident," she whispered. "That's all."

He lifted her hand and kissed her palm. "Not everyone would be so forgiving. Sandra wasn't." He looked into her eyes. "Did you write me?"

"Yes." Her voice broke. "Oh, Linc, I wanted to see you so much, to hear your voice, to have you hold me when I woke up cold and shaking. I was so alone . . ."

He folded her into his arms, holding her as though he would make the lonely years vanish. "I never should have let you go. I wanted to keep you so badly."

"Why didn't you?" she asked in a muffled voice.

"Sandra," he said simply. "She couldn't believe that I felt anything more than lust for you."

"She thought that of every man," said Holly curtly. "She was right most of the time, but she was wrong about you."

He smiled and kissed her nose. "I wanted your tender little body, Holly. But that wasn't all I wanted. I'd watched you, watched your parents. They loved each other and they loved you." He looked down and saw her confusion. "Don't give me that of-course-they-loved-me look. Living together doesn't necessarily mean loving together."

She remembered the rumors she had heard about his mother and stepmother—and his father who drank too much before he finally died. Then she realized that Sandra must have intercepted the letters she and Linc had sent to each other. She and Sandra had never been close, but Holly had not thought her aunt would lie to her. "Sandra has a lot to answer for," she said flatly.

He looked down at her eyes. They were hard and narrow, showing an anger that was repeated in the tight line of her mouth. "Don't blame her too much," he said. "When she first saw you, your face was swollen from crying, your hair was every which way and you were curled up in my arms asleep. You looked no more than thirteen. If you were mine and some hard-looking man said he was going to marry you, I'd have done the same thing Sandra did—scream and swear and generally raise enough hell to get us hustled out of the hospital."

"Maybe. But you wouldn't steal mail. And neither would I."

His lips flattened. "No, but I'm not surprised that she did. If there's one thing Dad taught me, it's that you can't trust beautiful women." He shrugged impatiently. "Sandra's a bitch, but no one can say she isn't beautiful."

Holly felt cold as she looked at his face. It was the cruel face of the stranger who had watched Shannon the way a cat watches a butterfly hovering over a blossom.

"Beauty doesn't have anything to do with it," she said quickly. "I know ugly women who are mean right to their marrow, and beautiful women who are kind."

His hand stroked her face tenderly. "You'd see kindness in a rattlesnake, *niña*," he said in a soft voice.

Holly felt a curious melting in her bones. Once she had hated it when he called her *niña*, "little one," but now the word was as sweet and warm to her as his lips.

"Kind Sandra," he continued, but his voice was different now, raw with remembered rage, "kind Sandra swore she wasn't going to let her sister's baby girl marry the son of an alcoholic and a whore, a man who knew nothing about love. So she waited until I was at my stepmother's funeral, and then she stole away the only person who might have taught me about love. Very kind, wouldn't you say? And so like a beautiful woman."

"Linc," said Holly, her voice ragged with his pain and her own fear. He looked so unyielding. "It's past. She can't take me away again."

He gathered her against his body with a strength that left her aching. "She'd better not even try. Did she come with you?"

"She stayed in Manhattan. Summer is a busy season for Sandra Productions. Everyone is shooting the spring line." She smiled at his blank look. "Clothes. In order to have all the ad campaigns ready for spring, they have to shoot in the summer."

Comprehension came, tightening his face into lines of distaste. "Yeah, I remember now. She makes her living selling skin to magazines."

"Linc!"

He saw the horrified look on her face. "Sorry." He sighed and ran his hand through his hair. Sunlight gleamed off his naked arm. "I don't like models," he said finally. "My mother and stepmother were both models. At least, that's what they called it. Looked like something else to me."

Holly closed her eyes and wished she didn't have to open her mouth and see her dream die again. But she couldn't lie to him, not even in silence. "I'm a model, Linc."

"What?"

"I'm a model." She opened her eyes, expecting to see contempt. Instead, she saw disbelief and amusement.

"A model," he said neutrally.

"Yes."

He laughed softly, looking her over from her rumpled

braid to her wrinkled cotton pants and sturdy shoes. "What do you model? Teddy bears? Swing sets? All-day suckers?"

For a moment she was angry that he still didn't recognize her as the glamorous model called Shannon. "I didn't realize I was so unattractive," she said in a clipped voice.

Linc's laughter vanished. He looked at her again, but this time his eyes remembered Holly as she had been in his arms, her body changing with each touch, her naked skin glowing with desire. "If you were any more beautiful," he said distinctly, "I would be afraid to trust you. Or myself."

"Being beautiful doesn't mean being untrustworthy," she said. "Beauty is just something done with mirrors and makeup. I can be beautiful and still be worth loving!"

"Hey, hey," he said, hugging her against his chest. "I wasn't talking about you, niña."

"But I was! I'm—"

Her words were lost beneath the sweetness of his tongue inside her mouth. His kiss told her of gentleness and caring and the passion for her that permeated his every breath. She moved with unconscious arousal, fitting herself against his body until there was nothing between them but clothes and the words he hadn't let her speak.

"You're more than beautiful enough for me," he said against her lips. "No," he said, filling her mouth again, making it impossible for her to speak. "No more arguments about beauty and women. We should know each other better before we argue. Please? I've just found you again, Holly. Let's not do anything to spoil it." He nipped her lips lightly. "Promise?"

"But—"

His mouth closed over hers, drawing out her breath in a single powerful kiss. "Promise me, Holly. Having you back is a dream come true. Just a few days. Just a

few days and then we can rant and rave and slang at
each other like old marrieds.''

"But—"

"I'm not a fool," he said quickly, cutting off her
words. "I know we'll fight." His eyes laughed down at
hers. "You always were a stubborn wench. But just for a
few days . . . ?"

"How many days?"

He smiled ruefully. "Like I said, a stubborn wench.
Two? That will get us past the Arabian Nights party at
the ranch. Then if you want to go fifty rounds, so be it."

Holly wavered, tempted. Then she shook her head.
"You'd be furious at me," she said softly, "when you
found out."

"Found out?" He stiffened. His fingers dug painfully
into her arms. "Found out what? *Are you married?*"

She stared at him speechlessly.

"Are you?" he demanded.

"Do you think I'd have touched you if I were
married?"

"Other women have," he said dryly.

"Not this one," she snapped. Then, sarcastically,
"Aren't you going to ask about fiancés, boyfriends and
lovers?"

His face changed, becoming a mask once more. "Are
there many?"

"Not a single one!" she exploded, words tumbling
out of her. "In fact, I'm a—" She stopped and looked
away, embarrassed by what she had almost said.

His expression shifted subtly, alive again. "You're a
what?" he coaxed.

Her chin lifted in a defiant gesture. She put her hands
on her hips, unconsciously echoing the moment yesterday when she had faced his contempt as Shannon. "I'm
not very experienced with men. But that shouldn't
surprise you. As you pointed out, I'm so damn *plain*."
She spun away and stalked back toward camp.

" Like I said, we should declare a truce for two days,"

he muttered, sweeping her off her feet. His lips moved over her ear, tickling it, making it hard for her to think. "Is that so unreasonable? Surely you can keep your temper that long?"

"But—"

"Damn it, woman, what does it take to convince you?"

"I just don't want you to hate me later."

"I could never hate you, *niña*. Don't you know that?"

"But you don't know me."

He glanced at the sky in exasperation. "That's the idea of the truce, remember?" He looked down at her. "Trust me, Holly. I'll be very gentle with you. I've waited so long and I'm afraid of losing you again before I have a chance . . ."

She didn't resist the kiss that stole her breath, replacing it with his, or the tongue that touched every part of her mouth in mute pleading. When he lifted his head, she sighed and smoothed her cheek against his neck.

"Truce?" he asked hoarsely.

"Truce."

"Good," he said, setting off toward the tent, still carrying her in his arms.

"What are you doing?"

He looked down at her, surprised by the hint of nervousness in her voice. "I thought I'd put my clothes out to dry."

"Oh."

Suddenly he stopped. "You said you hadn't had much experience . . . are you a virgin, Holly?"

"You make it sound like terminal acne."

"Are you or aren't you?"

"Does it matter?" she retorted. "This is the last half of the twentieth century, you know."

"I know. That's why I'm asking. You didn't act like a virgin," he said bluntly.

"Sorry about that," she said flippantly. "Chalk it up to false advertising. I'm as virgin as they come."

He stared at her angry face in frank surprise. "My God. Don't they have any men in New York?"

"Crawling with them."

"Well?"

"They weren't you, Linc."

She felt a tremor move through him. His lips brushed over her eyes, her mouth, her forehead, kisses so gentle she couldn't stop the upwelling of emotion that transformed her eyelashes into black nets glimmering with captive tears.

"I don't deserve you," he said huskily.

Her lips trembled into a smile. "You're stuck with me."

He held her for a long moment, his eyes closed, letting her words and her presence sink into him like water into dry land. Then he eased her down his body until her feet touched the ground once more.

"I'll get Dancer. You get dressed," he said.

"Aren't we going to—to—dry your clothes?" She sensed a flush creeping up her face and swore aloud. She felt like she should be digging a bare toe in the dirt, chewing on her braid and saying brilliant things like "Aw, shucks." Linc had a way of cutting through the sophisticated shell she had built around herself that was as maddening as it was . . . reassuring.

His thumb traced the high, slanting line of her cheekbone and smoothed the silky arch of her eyebrow. "Get dressed, *niña*," he whispered, "before my good intentions go down in flames."

Holly studied him. "Just because I'm a virgin?"

"Yes."

"It's a curable condition," she pointed out reasonably.

"No arguments, remember?"

Her eyes darkened. "I wouldn't dream of arguing with you. We'll *discuss* it over breakfast."

Giving him her best Shannon smile, she turned and walked back to the tent. Inside, it was warm and filled with golden light that seeped through pores in the canvas. She unzipped her pants and kicked them aside, smiling to herself as she wondered what Linc would have said if he had discovered that she had no underwear beneath her jeans.

The jacket zipper was as stubborn as ever. She peered at it, saw that it was hopelessly off track and slipped the jacket down over her hips. She stood naked for a moment, remembering how Linc had looked in the light pouring through the open tent flap. She felt a stirring in her body that was becoming familiar, fine wires tightening, teasing her with their promise of sensations she had not yet felt.

And, according to Linc, was not going to feel. She muttered a word that wasn't a normal part of her conversation and reached for her underwear.

Her bra was made of indigo lace, as were her bikini briefs. The blue-black color made her skin glow like dark honey, but she was in no temper to appreciate the sensual contrast between lace and skin. She yanked on her jeans and buttoned the rumpled blue chambray blouse all the way to the top. If he wanted a virgin, she'd give him a virgin. On a platter, hot and steaming, garnished with sage.

The image made her smile, then laugh at herself. She straightened the clutter inside the tent with the efficient motions of an experienced camper. On the way out, she grabbed the canteen and the firewood she had stored in the tent.

She started the fire with the same lack of fuss that had characterized her actions in the tent. When the flames had eaten solidly into the wood, she balanced a metal grate on the stones that surrounded the fire. She filled a bright new coffee pot and set it on the grate. Next, she filled the mess kit's biggest pot with water and put it next to the coffee. Finally, she picked up the latrine shovel and set off into the brush.

"The tent is ready when you are," she called over her shoulder. She couldn't see Linc but knew he was nearby, probably giving Sand Dancer a rough grooming with a handful of sage.

Linc's answering shout came from the direction of the springs.

She returned to camp carrying an armload of wood balanced on top of the ice chest she had retrieved from the Jeep. A tarp had kept everything reasonably dry. A second trip took care of the rest of the equipment she needed. She draped bacon in a small skillet and put it on the grate. After adding a few more sticks to the fire, she got up and hung wet clothes on the ropes that supported the tent.

Soon the twin smells of coffee and bacon were tormenting her. She looped the last of her wet underwear over a rope and hurried back to the fire. As she turned the bacon, Linc came into camp. He carried a saddle over his shoulder and a saddle blanket in his left hand. He flipped the blanket onto a tent rope. The motion sent a piece of her wet underwear fluttering down like an exotic bird. He caught the bit of scarlet lace on his fingertip and looked over his shoulder at her.

"Yours?"

"Couldn't be," she said placidly, turning the last piece of bacon. "I'm a virgin. Must be yours."

He laughed and slipped the saddle off his shoulder onto a boulder. She couldn't help noticing the resilient play of muscle, the easy grace of his movements, his casual acceptance of his physical strength.

"Bacon is burning," he said without turning around, knowing that she was watching him.

She gave the bacon a startled look. It wasn't even crisp yet. "No, it isn't."

"Funny," he said, hanging her briefs over the tent rope with elaborate care, "I could have sworn I smelled something burning. Do virgins burn, *niña?*"

His voice was low, as sensual as his fingers smoothing the scarlet lace. A liquid heat spread through her. She looked up, saw him studying her, waiting for her answer.

"Yes," she said.

"Good," he said softly. "But I'm going to wait until you're as hungry as I am."

"One, two, three." She snapped her fingers. "That's it. I'm as hungry as you are." She came to her feet in one graceful motion and started for the tent.

Laughing, he vanished inside the tent and held the flap shut. "Bacon's burning."

"I like it that way," she said, tugging at the flap.

Just then, bacon grease spattered noisily as flames licked over the edge of the frying pan. She threw a frustrated look at the tent and ran back to the fire, rescuing the bacon from certain incineration. A few deft pokes with a stick knocked down the fire. She opened a loaf of bread and put five slices to toast on the grate. The cooked bacon went into one of the two plates that had come with the mess kit. The coffee perked companionably, almost ready to drink.

"How many eggs and what way?" she called, not looking up.

"Three. Over easy."

His voice was close, unexpected. Fingers traced the line of her chin and teased the curve of her ear. She turned and rubbed her lips over his palm, then bit the pad of flesh at the base of his thumb with just enough force to be felt through the callus. He drew in his breath swiftly. When he spoke, his voice was as smoky as his eyes.

"You keep that up and I'll trip you and beat you to the ground."

"Promises, promises," she murmured. Her tongue flicked out to the sensitive skin between his fingers. "You taste better than bacon."

"Holly," he said thickly, "you promised not to argue."

"Who's arguing?"

He took her hand and held it to his lips. His tongue retraced every pathway hers had taken before he let her go. She turned the bread with quick motions, wondering what he had been doing in the tent, for he still wore his wet jeans. She glanced quickly at the tent ropes. A pair of navy men's briefs hung next to her bright bra.

"Butter in the ice chest," she said. "Honey, too."

She broke eggs into the bacon pan, poured two cups of coffee and laid most of the crisp bacon on his plate. She flipped the eggs deftly, counted to ten and slid them onto his plate. Three of the five pieces of toast went on top.

Holly cooked two more eggs, reached for her toast and saw that Linc had prepared it for her. A rich sheen of butter and honey swirled over the bread and dripped over the crust to make tiny golden beads on her plate. Though she ate quickly, he finished far ahead of her. He poured another cup of coffee and squatted on his heels next to the rock she had chosen for a chair.

"You're amazing, *niña*," he said, sipping the coffee.

"Yeah. Right," she said, licking honey off her fingers. "Not too many geriatric virgins these days."

He chuckled. "That's not what I meant. First you drag me to shelter, take care of me, then go back out and risk your neck taking care of my crazy horse. I wake up in the morning and think I'm still dreaming because there's the taste of you on my lips. Then . . ." He sighed and sipped gingerly at the coffee, his hazel eyes taking in the campsite. "Later, I'm gone for fifteen minutes rubbing down a horse and I come back to find the tent organized, a fire going, breakfast waiting and sexy lingerie hanging next to my socks."

He took her hand and rubbed his moustache against it. With a gentle squeeze, he released her fingers. "You have no idea what a shining pleasure it is not to be saddled with a gorgeous, useless woman. I don't remember my mother ever cooking up anything but goop for facials, and my stepmother was even worse. They wouldn't have been able to set up a tent, much less know how to trench around it. They wouldn't have gone out in a storm to take care of a horse. Hell," he said, his voice suddenly cold, "they wouldn't go out in a drizzle to save their own children. But they'd crawl naked through cactus to a cheap motel."

He stared out over the fire, seeing only the cold past.

Holly set down her empty plate. She put her hand on his bare shoulder, blending her warmth with his. "I'm sorry they hurt you."

The beard stubble on his cheek rasped lightly over her hand. "It's over and done with."

"Is it? You still hate beautiful women." His cheek lifted abruptly off her hand. Displeasure showed clearly in the tightness of his mouth. It was a subject he was not willing to discuss. But it was too important to ignore in the futile hope that it would never come up again. It would, and the longer she waited, the worse it would be. "Would your mother's and stepmother's selfishness have been any easier to bear if they had been ugly?"

"If they had been ugly, they wouldn't have been selfish." His voice was smooth and cold, leaving no opening for disagreement. It was as though he had just said that the sun set in the West. A fact, indisputable.

Holly started to speak, then thought better of it. Linc had been hurt by actions, not words. It would take actions, not words, to convince him that not all beautiful women were selfish and cruel. She had made a start just by being herself, by caring for him and his horse. She had not planned it that way; it was simply her. She could no more hide her basic nature than she could step out of her skin. She was beautiful, but she wasn't cruel. In time, he had to see that.

She was glad that she had agreed to a truce. She only hoped two days would be enough.

5

Holly rubbed the skillet with sand, wrapped it in newspaper and stacked it in the supply carton. She carried the carton to the Jeep along with the tarp that had covered Dancer. Though it was not yet ten o'clock, the sun cut through her thin blouse like a laser. The sky was blue-white, bright with water vapor, and even now the first clouds were forming against the highest peaks. By evening, summer thunder would come again to the dry land, bringing the gift of water.

From habit she moved quietly, listening to the desert sounds. Quail whistled from beneath the chaparral. Brush rubbed over itself with a soft, leathery sound. Bees hummed endlessly, frantic with their efforts to take advantage of the brief bloom that followed unexpected rain.

The unusual weather had unsettled the desert inhabitants. Many of them lived underground, letting the land itself insulate them from the sun's killing heat. The hard rains had filled holes and burrows with water, driving the animals up to the surface. There they would stay until the water sank beneath the level of their homes. In the rainy season the land softened and allowed water to drain quickly out of the burrows. In the summer it took longer, for the land had been baked like clay in a kiln.

At the Jeep, she shifted the gas can aside to make room for the carton. Metal clanged against metal. In the silence that followed, the dry buzz of a rattlesnake sounded very loud.

For an instant she was thirteen again, taking a shortcut through her backyard to the corral. She hadn't heard the rattlesnake then, but she had seen it strike, sinking its fangs into her leg. Her jeans and thick socks had protected her, but not enough to prevent some of the poison from entering her blood. The venom had been like molten metal burning through her. She had screamed in agony then because she couldn't help herself.

She was screaming now, remembering.

"Holly!"

Linc was shaking her, calling her name again and again. With a convulsive shudder, she returned to the present.

"I'm all right," she said hoarsely.

"What happened?"

"Rattlesnake." She laughed shakily. "It's gone now. It probably was as scared as I was."

Linc knelt and yanked up her pant legs, looking for puncture wounds left by fangs.

"It wasn't close enough to strike," she said, trying to stop shaking. "I feel like such a fool. There are always snakes around the springs. I shouldn't have been so surprised."

Linc finished checking her legs and stood. He looked at her white lips, at the sweat that stood out on her skin. "Even if the snake had bitten you, I have antivenin in the saddlebag."

"I was bitten when I was thirteen. I'm allergic to the venom. I'm even more allergic to the antivenin. Dad barely got me to the hospital in time. When I came to the next day, the doctor told me that unless I happened to be in an emergency ward the next time a rattler bit me, I would die."

"Then why in the name of God did you come to the springs?" said Linc, fear making his voice harsh.

Holly smiled, though her lips were still pale. "Lots of people have the same problem with bee stings, but they don't stay shut up in their houses. I just have to remember where I am, and then I won't panic if I see another rattler. At least," she added honestly, "I hope I won't."

"New rules, Holly."

She looked up, surprised by the seriousness in his voice.

"You don't walk or ride anywhere in the desert alone," continued Linc, measuring her reaction. "When you do go out, you go second, not first. Let somebody else find the snakes."

Her first impulse was to argue. Her second was to agree with his common sense approach. He wasn't telling her she had to stay locked in a house. He was simply trying to work out a safe way for her to enjoy the desert she loved.

Smiling, she waved toward camp. "After you, *monsieur.*"

"Agreeable, aren't you?" he said, surprised.

"Uh-huh. Docile, loyal and obedient, too. Want to scratch my ears?"

Linc laughed. "You're full of surprises, Holly. There was a time when you would have raised hell if I told you to do something sensible."

"I'm not sixteen anymore." She looked up at him with eyes that were almost gold. "Six years, Linc. I've changed in a lot of ways. I can be very beautiful. Will you still want me when you realize that?"

His eyes narrowed. "Do you think I don't know how—" He took a deep breath, shutting off his irritation. "You're a warm, capable, stubborn woman. Very warm. Very woman. And very damn stubborn." He shook his head in rueful amusement. "And I'm glad you aren't sixteen, *niña*. I'm having a bad enough time with my conscience as it is."

"You make me wish I wasn't a virgin," she said sadly.

"Why?" His tongue parted her lips with deep, slow strokes that brought a low sound out of her throat. When he lifted his mouth, his eyes were brilliant with desire. "Just kissing you is more exciting than sleeping with another woman."

For an instant the image of Cyn's voluptuous, experienced body flashed before Holly's eyes. She stiffened.

Linc felt the change in her. He held her at arm's length. "What's wrong?"

"Another woman," she said, trying to make her voice light. "How can I compete with Cyn, being a plain virgin and all? And you so damned handsome . . ." Holly looked away from his intense hazel eyes.

"Cyn! Who told you about her? Look at me, Holly."

Reluctantly, Holly turned her head. Linc's expression was gentle and intent. His eyes searched hers. "Cyn and I had an arrangement that was mutually convenient."

"Had?" whispered Holly, remembering Cyn's full breasts and hips pressed against his body, his arm around her, his eyes amused and indulgent. And those same eyes so scornful of the woman called Shannon.

"Had," said Linc firmly. "You're all I want, Holly. You're more than I dreamed I'd ever have."

"Then why won't you make love to me?"

He smiled crookedly. "I have."

"You know what I mean."

"Is being a virgin so terrible?" he teased.

"Not terrible. Painful. I ache, Linc."

He drew in his breath sharply. Passion burned behind his thick lashes. "You're getting there."

"Getting where?"

"To the point where you're as hungry as I am."

She groaned. "You mean it gets worse?"

"Much worse. And then it gets much, much better."

"Worse? That isn't possible."

"Isn't it?"

His fingers slowly unbuttoned her blouse. As the soft blue folds parted, he smoothed the fabric off her shoulders. For a long moment he simply looked at her. Her breath shortened in answer to the desire that leaped in his eyes. Heat spread beneath her skin, making it glow. Beneath the indigo bra her nipples tightened, aroused simply by his look.

Fingertips stroked her throat, cherishing the pulse that beat visibly beneath her flesh. She watched his face, watched his eyes grow smoky, his lips part in a sensuous smile, his tongue move between his teeth. Wires tightened all through her, making her tremble, and he had done nothing more than look at her and touch the life beating in her throat.

He slid the blouse down her arms and over her hands, biting her fingertips as they emerged from the blue sleeves. She closed her eyes, caught in the sensuality that radiated from him like heat from the sun.

"Look at my hands," he whispered against her lips, taking her mouth in a kiss that was as deep as it was quick.

Her black lashes lifted. She saw his hands, brown and strong and very male against the delicate lace of her bra. She changed beneath his hands. When his nails raked lightly over her nipples, her breath stopped, then started again, more quickly. She watched his hands, fascinated by their beauty, held by his lightest touch more surely than if she had been chained.

With dreamlike slowness, his hand curved around her breast. He caught her nipple between his thumb and finger, rubbing lightly. She arched against his hand, tormented by a touch that was too light and too knowing. He bent and took her nipple between his teeth, making her gasp with pleasure.

He lifted his head almost immediately. His hands moved over the front fastening of her bra. It came undone, yet indigo lace still clung to the fullness of her breasts. His long finger slipped beneath the lace, peeling it off slowly, watching her with eyes more green than brown, intense with passion.

She saw his lips close over her, felt her nipple harden as his tongue and lips tugged at her in a caress that made her moan. She held his head between her hands and succumbed to the heat that twisted through her, melting her. His teeth closed over her again, less gently this time, knowing she was too aroused to feel a light touch anymore. She made a fierce sound of pleasure and buried her fingers in his thick hair.

For a time he held her hard against him, taking as much pleasure from the desire that shook her as she did. Then his mouth gentled again, nibbling between her breasts, ignoring her sensitive nipples. He blew on her hot skin, teasing her until her nails dug into his arm in frustration.

"You're right," she breathed. "It's worse. Love me, Linc."

He laughed softly. "I said *much* worse."

Before she could protest, he took her mouth in a kiss that consumed her. His hands undid her jeans, easing the faded fabric down over her hips. He lifted her and pulled off the jeans, leaving her wearing only a wisp of indigo lace. His hands roamed over her skin, savoring her heat and the tremors of desire that quivered through her. His right hand moved over her lacy briefs, then slid beneath the elastic. Fingers rubbed lightly over her hot flesh, searched intimately, sliding into her.

She gasped and shuddered convulsively, gripped by intense, consuming pleasure. *"What are you doing to me?"*

"Not a tenth what I'd like to," he said thickly. "You're so soft . . ." His palm cupped around her, pressing against her while his fingers moved deeply. With a groan he knelt to kiss her shadowed softness.

"Linc—!"

Surprise and passion mingled equally in her voice. With a shudder he turned his head away and lay with his cheek on her stomach. For a minute he was rigid, fighting to control himself. He stood up swiftly.

"Sorry," he said, gathering her clothes, fastening her bra and pulling her blouse into place as he spoke. "I forgot that your virginity isn't just a technicality. No man has ever really touched you . . ." He handed over her jeans.

She dressed, too shaken by her unexpected feelings to argue. But as soon as her surprise passed, she wanted nothing more than to feel like that again, weak and strong, burning and melting, aching and ecstasy all wound together.

She helped him finish loading the Jeep and tie the tarp in place.

"Record time." He smiled. "We make quite a team."

She returned his smile and ran her finger over the edges of his moustache. "Took you long enough to find out," she said softly.

His eyes changed as he remembered just how well they did some things together. He reached for her, then caught himself. "We'll never get home that way."

"Depends on what you mean by 'home,'" she said.

"A bed with you in it." Linc took a last look at the sky. There was a blue-black density to the margin between cloud and land that told of mountain storms. "Antelope Wash looks like a bad risk. We'll both ride Dancer out. I can send my men to pick up your stuff tomorrow."

"I can pick it up after the shoot on Monday." The instant the words were out of her mouth she regretted them.

"Them!" His voice was scornful. "The tame Viking and his black-haired whore." He saw her stricken expression and controlled his tongue. "I forgot. You're with them. Of all the mismatches—" He shook his head and forced a smile.

Tears and anger and fear twisted her throat, squeezing her voice. "Royce models are just that—models. I'm one of them."

Linc heard her emotion more than her words. He hugged her. "I'd make a terrible diplomat," he said against her black hair, "breaking my own truces and saying all the wrong things. The last thing I want to do is hurt you. Truce? Again?"

"You're wrong about Roger's models," she said urgently.

"I'm wrong about Roger's models," he repeated dutifully. "Truce?"

She knew he hadn't changed his mind, knew that words alone weren't enough. "Truce," she said evenly. "But someday I'm really going to have to rearrange your prejudices."

He smiled thinly. "It took a lifetime to arrange them."

"And all I have is two days . . ."

"You have a lifetime, *niña,* if you want it."

"Do I?"

He sensed her despair, though he didn't understand its cause. He held her in a fierce grip, trying to banish the fear he saw in her eyes. She leaned against him, glorying in the rasp of beard stubble against her cheek. Her hands slid up his back, holding him with a woman's surprising strength. They stood for a long time, pressed tightly together, each storing up the other's presence like land drinking water after a long drought.

The Mountains of Sunrise had changed little in the six years since Holly had last seen Linc's ranch. The white fences around the house, show-rings and paddocks were as clean as the clouds gathering against the mountains. The irrigated pastures were green, the grazing horses were sleek and lively. On either side were other ranches—Garner Valley was famous for horses. The valley lay between two ridges of the San Jacinto Mountains. The contrast between the sand-and-rock desert and the pine-and-grass valley was startling.

A big yellow dog came trotting out from the barn and stood near Dancer, waving a thick tail in greeting.

"Hello, Freedom," said Linc, sliding off Sand Dancer and scratching the dog's ears. "Did you lose Beth?"

Holly dismounted, collecting a wet lick from Freedom as soon as her feet hit the ground.

"Beth will be glad to see you. She missed you almost as much as I did," he said. "She's at the age when all her friends stay in town. She'd rather be at our Palm Springs house."

"It must be lonely for her."

"Don't you start in on me." Then he sighed. "Sorry. Beth and Mrs. Malley keep harping on how much nicer it is in Palm Springs. But Mrs. Malley can't keep Beth on a short enough leash."

"Beth used to love the ranch," said Holly.

"That was before she discovered boys. Now all she can think about is painting her face and buying flashy clothes."

"It's normal at fifteen," she said, touching his arm.

"You weren't like that," he said bluntly.

"I was a tomboy. Is Beth doing well at school? Are her friends wild?"

"She's a straight-A student. Her girl friends wear too much paint, but they're nice-enough kids."

"Then you're worrying over nothing."

"I hope so." He rubbed his hand through his hair in a gesture of frustration that was becoming familiar to Holly. Then his mouth flattened into an unyielding line. "Some days she reminds me so much of her mother it scares me. But she won't end up like that if I have to lock her in her room and eat the key."

The back door of the house slammed and a girl nearly as tall as Holly came running toward them. Holly recognized Beth by the long, honey-colored braids that streamed behind her.

"Holly! Is it really you?" She threw herself into Holly's arms. "I always told Linc you'd come back! Where did you come from? How did Linc find you? Why were you riding double? Are you back to stay? Did—"

Laughing, Linc put his hand over Beth's mouth. "Slow down, Button."

"Button!" she said hotly. "I'm nearly *sixteen!*"

Holly looked at Beth's clean, shining face and felt like a lump of mud. "I'll flip you for the bathtub," she said to Linc.

"We could share," he offered.

Holly threw a startled glance at Beth. The younger girl looked surprised, then pleased. "You can use my bubble bath."

Smiling, Holly shook her head.

"Spoilsport," said Linc. He began leading Dancer toward the barn. "Use the master bath. Beth and I will take care of Dancer."

As they walked away, the girl's clear voice floated back. "Okay, big brother. Yesterday you rode out of here alone with a shirt and a saddle. Today you show up shirtless and bareback with Holly. Give."

The house was huge, clean and cool, decorated in earth tones that complemented the Navaho rugs that Linc's father had collected. The size of the master bathroom startled her. It was as big as her Manhattan apartment. The sunken bathtub—with Jacuzzi—was big enough to swim in. And like a swimming pool, it was kept full of warm water. Holly looked at it longingly, but could not bring herself to waste all that water just to clean one body.

A quick search of the bathroom turned up soap, shampoo and towel. She took off her clothes and stepped into the oversized shower. With a sigh of sheer pleasure, she let hot water pour over her, washing away the dust of the long ride up and over the ridge to the ranch.

She shook out a towel, then stood bemused. The towel was obviously made for Linc. It was longer than she was and twice as wide. Smiling, she rubbed herself dry, then took the unused half of the towel and went to work on her hair. When she was finished, she deftly French braided the sides and crown, blending the shorter hair around her face into a sleek cap and leaving the longer hair to dry in gentle waves down her back. She coaxed a few tendrils loose to soften the slanting lines of her eyes and cheekbones, frowned at the too-young, too-plain image in the mirror and wrapped the big towel several times around her. With dirty clothes in hand, she went to look for a washing machine.

"Just in time," she said as the bedroom door opened and Linc walked in.

"Looks more like too late to me." His hazel eyes took in the towel that covered her from collarbones to feet. "I was going to offer to scrub your back, among other things."

Holly hesitated. "What about Beth?"

"I don't think she wants to scrub you nearly as badly as I do," he said, deliberately misunderstanding. Then, softly, "Don't worry about Beth. She'd move heaven and earth to get you in my bed." He smiled at Holly's expression. "You look shocked that Beth knows about men, women and beds." He smiled thinly. "She grew up fast. With a mother like hers, she had to."

"I'm shocked that you'd bring your . . . playmates . . . to your home. No matter how mature Beth is, she might be uneasy having breakfast with your most recent acquisition."

"If I'm sleeping double, I sleep somewhere else," he said bluntly. "You'll be the first, *niña*. And the last." His fingers wound in her long black hair. He pulled her toward him and tilted her face to receive his lips. Just as his mouth touched hers he whispered, "Marry me, Holly."

Before she could answer, he pulled her against him, kissing her so thoroughly she could not breathe. She returned his kiss with a passionate abandon that made both of them tremble.

"I won't hear anything except yes," he said, his eyes clear and very certain. "So if you want to argue, you'll just have to wait until after the party. Truce, remember?"

She wanted to say yes more than she had ever wanted to do anything in her life. She had always known that she loved Linc. Now she was learning just how much. But until he knew she was Shannon, she couldn't make promises he might not want to keep. "I'll wait until our truce ends to say yes."

Linc's face became very still. "Why wait if it's yes?"

"When the truce ends, you may want to withdraw the offer."

"You think we'll have a horrible fight right away?" he asked, smiling crookedly.

"I know we will," she said, unsmiling. "But if you want me afterward, you've got me."

He slid his fingers between the towel and her breast. "Do I have to wait that long?" he said, squeezing gently.

She drew in a quick breath. "Only for the answer. The woman you could have had anytime since dawn."

Beth's voice came down the hallway. "Linc?"

Slowly he withdrew his hand, but otherwise made no move to separate himself from her. "In here, Beth."

Beth breezed into the room, saw Linc with his arms around Holly, and grinned. "Does this mean that after six years I'm finally going to have Holly as a sister?"

"I'm working on it," sighed Linc. "She's damn near as stubborn as I am."

"Try one of your famous truces," retorted Beth.

"I did. Midnight tomorrow, she says yes."

Beth whooped and threw her arms around both Holly and Linc. "Oh boy, just like Cinderella!"

Holly smiled wryly. Midnight hadn't been Cinderella's finest hour.

6

~~~~~~~~~~~

"Linc said to tell you he'll be in the barn for a while. It's the mare's first foal, and she can't decide whether to lie down and have it or stand around and look surprised. It could be all night."

Holly sighed and buttoned her freshly washed blouse and tested her hair. It was dry enough to braid.

"You make it look so easy," said Beth.

"Mmmm?" said Holly absently, fingers weaving in deft patterns.

"Your braid. It looks so smart." She held up one of her own with disgust. "Pigtails or ponytails. Yck."

"There are other things you can do with long hair if you don't want to cut it."

"I do want to cut it, but Linc won't let me. No makeup, no neat clothes and the same hair I had six years ago." Beth's full mouth twisted into a grimace. "I didn't mind for a while, but now—"

"A boy?" asked Holly.

Beth smiled shyly and nodded her head. "Jack. My best friend's older brother."

"If he's worth your time, he won't care about your clothes or hair."

Beth looked stubborn. "That's what Linc says."

"Maybe he's right."

"Maybe. But why do *I* have to be the one to test *his* theories? Besides," she added bitterly, "when Linc goes out, he sure doesn't pick the plain ones!"

"You aren't plain," said Holly quickly.

The younger girl turned and looked at Holly with level eyes. "Yes, I am. Oh, my teeth are straight and my skin is clear and my figure is okay. Nice enough, but no second looks."

Holly measured Beth as though seeing her for the first time. Her eyes were the lambent, pale turquoise of a rainwashed desert sky. Her lips were full, ready to smile or pout or laugh. Her skin was smooth, tanned and glowing with health. With a discreet amount of makeup, the right clothes and another hairstyle . . .

"Holly?" Beth waved her hand in front of Holly's face. "Anybody home?"

"Come on," said Holly, holding out her hand. "If we hurry, we'll have an hour before the shops close in Palm Springs." As she stood up, Holly glanced in the mirror. Blue shirt and faded blue jeans. Clodhopper shoes and no makeup. She barely looked old enough to drive. She shook her head. "If Roger sees me like this, he'll disown me."

"Who's Roger?" said Beth.

"My boss."

"Oh . . . what kind of work do you do?"

"I'm a model."

Beth took a quick breath. "Does Linc know?"

"Yes," she said grimly, "but he doesn't really believe it."

"Holly—" Beth swallowed. "He hates models," she said in a strained voice. "His mother and mine were both models."

"I know." She smiled at Beth with a cheerfulness she didn't feel. "Ready to go shopping?"

Holly drove one of Linc's cars, a bronze BMW coupe that was built for twisting mountain roads. The air was sultry. Vague hints of thunder muttered among the clouds and mountaintops. Once in Palm Springs, Holly let Beth choose the store.

Chez Elegance was a small, exclusive shop that featured clothes suitable for teenagers as well as women over twenty. Holly was relieved to see that even the most avant-garde designs depended on quality rather than shock for their impact.

At the front door, Beth paused. "This is my favorite store, but Linc never lets me buy anything here."

"Too expensive?"

"Too 'advanced.' "

"Trust me," Holly said crisply. "When I'm through, you won't look like any more than you are—or any less."

An hour later they came out of the shop with a loose, off-white silk blouse and a floor-length silk skirt of the same pale turquoise as Beth's eyes. There were thin, matching ribbons to braid into her hair. Silver sandals with modest heels completed the outfit.

Beth was ecstatic. As soon as they were out on the sidewalk, she clutched the packages to her and whirled around and around, crowing her delight. "What a wonderful homecoming present, Holly! I can't wait for the party! Jack's coming with his parents! Wait until he sees me! He'll—" She stopped abruptly as she bumped into someone.

"Watch those big feet of yours," snapped Cyn.

Holly and Beth turned around as one. "Sorry," mumbled Beth.

"There's nothing wrong with Beth's feet," said Holly coolly. "She handles them better than you do your tongue."

Cyn's narrowed eyes took in Holly's blouse and jeans and shoes. "A new ranch hand?" she said, turning to Beth.

The girl smiled with pure malice. "Didn't Linc tell you this morning when he called from the barn? Holly is going to be Mrs. Lincoln McKenzie."

Cyn's face changed, older now, and much harder. "Listening in on the extension again? I'm not surprised. Plain girls have to be sly. They have nothing else going for them."

Beth tried to hide how much Cyn's words hurt, but could not. She simply wasn't old enough to match put-downs with someone like Cyn.

"If you'd ever take out those dark-blue contact lenses," said Holly distinctly, "you'd notice that Beth is beautiful."

Cyn's laughter was as light and delicate as her perfume. "You've got to be kidding. She's almost as plain as you are. Haven't you heard—men like their women soft, tiny and round."

"Especially in the heels?" smiled Holly.

Cyn turned on her like a cat. "Just because you saved Linc's life doesn't mean he wants you," she said in a voice that crackled with anger. "He'll get tired of your plain Jane innocence fast enough. He's all man. And face it, sweetie. You have the sex appeal of a concrete slab."

"Concrete slab?" murmured Holly. Her eyes were narrowed and every bit as hard as Cyn's. "Come to the Arabian Nights ball, Cyn. Watch men stand in line to talk to me. And then I'll watch you wish you'd never been so blind and bitchy as to call Beth plain. Got that, *sweetie?*"

Cyn stared at her for a moment in disbelief. "You couldn't get your mirror to look at you, much less a man."

"Prove it," shot back Holly.

"I'm coming to the ball," said Cyn, "but the men will

be looking at me, not you." The sound of her laughter drifted on the air even after she was halfway down the block.

"I hate her," said Beth in a strained voice. "I don't know what Linc sees in her."

Holly grimaced. She knew exactly what Linc saw in Cyn. "He's accustomed to her . . . face."

"Sorry," sighed Beth, touching her arm. "You didn't have to crawl out on a limb for me. I know I'm plain."

"You are not plain," she said, emphasizing each word. Then guessing the source of Beth's concern, Holly gave her a wink. "Come on. Let's go to the hotel and pick up my stuff. You're going to be almost as surprised as Cyn when I do my caterpillar-to-butterfly act."

But nobody was going to be as surprised as Linc when Shannon rather than Holly came to the ball. She frowned uncomfortably at the thought. A gust of hot, humid wind washed over her, smelling of sand and rain. Beth and Holly ran to the car.

They just beat the storm home. As Holly pulled into the driveway, lightning stitched through the clouds overhead.

"Linc?" called Holly, as she walked into the kitchen.

No one answered.

"Still in the foaling barn, I'll bet," said Beth, heading for her bedroom, packages in hand. She stopped in the hall. "Are you sure you won't let me pay you back? Daddy left me money in my own name."

"It's my homecoming present for you."

"It's an awfully expensive present . . ."

"Don't worry, every penny of it is going to come out of Sandra's hide."

"Yeah, Linc told me about that. What a witch. She even kept *my* letter from getting to you."

Holly's smile vanished. Without it, she looked remote, unapproachable. "You wrote to me, too?"

"Sure. Except for Linc, you were the only one who ever loved me."

Holly crossed the kitchen to hug Beth, packages and all. "I still love you. And I wrote to you."

Beth's eyes were bright with emotion as she returned the hug. "I love you, too. I wish Sandra had never come. Linc would have been happier and so would I." Her lips quirked. "I'll bet I'd have been an aunt by now."

And Shannon would never have been born, thought Holly.

The idea disturbed her. At first, the Shannon persona had made her uneasy; that was why she had chosen to work under another name. But the name itself was part of her—her middle name, her mother's maiden name. Shannon. From the beginning, Shannon had grown out of Holly's own needs, whether she admitted it at the time or not.

Whatever Holly wasn't, Shannon was. Shannon had never been orphaned at sixteen. Shannon had never wept to be beautiful so that the man she loved would notice her. Shannon had never been awkward or too tall. Shannon had never been lonely. The list was endless.

Or was it? Shannon didn't fall in bed or love with the men who pursued her. Neither did Holly. Shannon didn't want to be petted or worn like a life-sized charm on a rich man's bracelet. Neither did Holly. Shannon dreamed of Linc, felt his skin beneath her palms, tasted him on her lips. So did Holly. Shannon was intelligent, hard-working and responsible. She wanted to be the best, and she was. She was the Royce Reflection.

And so was Holly.

She realized that slowly, imperceptibly, the two expressions of her personality had grown together. Or perhaps it was simply that she had grown up. She was finally able to accept herself without flinching. She was plain Holly and fancy Shannon . . . and so was every woman. But the essential inner person was the same no matter what the trappings, plain or fancy. The woman beneath the changing exterior was herself unchanging. And she loved and wanted to be loved by one man. Linc.

"Is the idea of children so boggling?" laughed Beth.

Holly blinked, called out of her own thoughts by Beth's question. She smiled. "I'd have to get Roger to design a line of maternity clothes."

"Roger designs clothes?"

"No more questions about my boss or my work until midnight tomorrow," Holly said quickly.

"Ask you no questions and you'll tell me no lies?" said Beth, smiling but tentative.

"I wouldn't lie to you. I haven't lied to Linc." She sighed and added softly, "I haven't told him all of the truth, either. But then, if he had twenty-twenty vision, I wouldn't have to!"

Holly carried her luggage and makeup case to the master bedroom. Beth came in and poked through the case while Holly unpacked. When she was finished, she turned to the girl. Beth was elbow deep in makeup, her expression divided between apology and stubbornness. Instead of saying anything, Holly sat down next to her on the bed.

"Well?" said Beth.

"Well what?"

"I like it," Beth said firmly, looking at herself in the case's mirrored lid.

Privately, Holly thought Beth looked wretched. Black eyebrows, black lashes, scarlet lips and cheeks. The makeup had been applied without thought to age, natural coloring or to the individual lines of Beth's face. Using makeup correctly, like speech, was a learned skill. No one was born with it.

"Let me try something," Holly said in a mild voice. She removed makeup from half of Beth's face, talking as she worked. "In class, we were told to put normal makeup on half our face. Then the teacher came around and made up the other half."

She worked quickly, her years of practice showing in each deft stroke. "Makeup is as individual as the person wearing it. What I'm using on you now would look odd on you at twenty-five, ridiculous at thirty-five and pathetic at forty-five. Each age has its own unique needs and beauty. But what I'm using now would look terrible on me at any age, just as my colors would look terrible on you. I'm dark. You're blond. I have brown eyes, you have blue. My nose is off-center, yours is snub. You have lovely full lips, I don't. My cheeks and eyes are too slanted—"

"Too slanted—" objected Beth. "There's no such thing."

Holly smiled. "My face is triangular, yours is oval. In short, we need different makeup to bring out our special qualities."

"I don't have any special qualities," said Beth gloomily.

"Sure you do. But you won't see them buried under piles of makeup." Holly worked in silence for a few more moments, concentrating on the mascara. She added a touch of blusher to bring out Beth's cheekbones, examined the results and nodded.

Beth grabbed the makeup case and lifted the lid. For a long time she studied the two halves of her face. "Boy," she said finally, "you know a lot more about makeup than I do." She grabbed tissue and cream and wiped off the makeup that Holly had not applied.

"There." Beth studied her face again, comparing the right side, the one with makeup, to the left side, which had none.

While Beth looked in the mirror, Holly undid the girl's right braid. She brushed the shining, waist-length hair until it was smooth. She pulled the hair back from Beth's face and began styling it in different ways. Finally she made loose French braids on the sides and crown to keep the hair from overwhelming Beth's face. The remainder of the hair was left free to fall in honey waves down the center of her back. The result was a simple yet sophisticated style that brought out the oval perfection of Beth's face.

"A shampoo and some hot rollers will take out the kinks from wearing pigtails. I have some earrings that will be perfect with your skirt." Holly became aware that Beth wasn't listening. "Beth?"

"Huh?" said Beth. Then she blinked as though waking up and tore her glance away from the mirror. "Is that really me?" she whispered. "My eyes look so *blue*. And big. And my hair— I even like my hair! What did you do to my cheekbones? I don't look like a kid anymore. How did you do it?"

"Yes," said a cold voice from the doorway, "tell me how you turned a sweet young kid into a tart."

Beth froze.

Holly kept her back to the door and spoke as though Linc were not there. "Hold the mirror, Beth," she said evenly. "I'll show you what I did."

She put her fingers under Beth's chin and turned the pigtailed, plain side of Beth toward Linc. He drew in a swift, hard breath as he measured the difference in the two halves of his sister's face. A closed look settled over him. For an instant he was a stranger again, glaring at a woman whose beauty offended him. Only the helpless pleading in Beth's eyes kept Holly from giving up right there. Willing her hand not to tremble, she began applying a sheer foundation to the left side of Beth's face.

"No!" said Linc. "You're making her look like a two-dollar—" He stopped abruptly, swearing beneath his breath.

Holly's hand paused, then continued with sure strokes. "Are you calling off our truce, Linc?" she asked, not looking up from Beth's face.

"If anyone is calling it off, you are."

She measured the result of the foundation, found that it matched the other side, and picked up the pale brown eyebrow pencil. "I'm not arguing," she said. "You are. I haven't even raised my voice."

It took every bit of Holly's professional poise to appear casual as she picked up pale turquoise eyeshadow and turned back to Beth. "A two-dollar floozy," said Holly evenly, "wears brassy makeup and puts it on with a trowel. This makeup is chosen for subtlety and there isn't a trowel in sight."

Linc's face became completely expressionless. He crossed his arms and leaned against the door. He looked unreasonably big. "Beauty is as beauty does," he said in a flat, hard voice.

"No argument there," said Holly, reaching for a pale eyeshadow to blend with the turquoise. "But you've done your best to keep Beth plain. Why? Don't you trust her?"

"What the hell is that supposed to mean?"

Beth stirred at the whiplash of her brother's voice. Holly pressed a hand over her arm, silently urging her to stay put.

"I mean," said Holly, "that you've chosen her clothes and hairstyle with an unerring eye toward hiding the beauty that is coming to her as she grows older. Do you hate beauty so much? Can't you see that even though the outside changes, the inside is still worthy of love? My God, Linc. You've raised her. She's like your own daughter."

"She's also her mother's daughter," said Linc, "and her mother was a slut."

"I hate you!" cried Beth.

She leaped up and ran out the door that connected the master suite to Linc's office. From there, they could hear the door to the hallway and then to her bedroom slam shut. With shaking hands, Holly packed up the case containing her cosmetics.

"Do you really think Beth is a slut?" she asked, her voice quivering with rage.

"Of course not!"

"Then when you both cool off, I suggest you tell her that." She snapped the case shut. She stood, holding the case protectively against her body. "And what about me?" she asked, her face drawn into unyielding lines. "When I get out of my childish clothes and hairstyles, when I put something more than soap on my face, will I become magically degraded in your eyes? Will a stylish dress and a few strokes of an eyebrow pencil turn me into a worthless, lying, cheating prostitute?"

"Holly—"

"Will it?" she said, her voice rising. "Beauty is as beauty does, right? Except, of course, where it interferes with your prejudices. Then no matter what beauty does, beauty is a beast."

"I thought we had a truce," he said coldly.

"I'll gamble my own future on a truce," shot back Holly, "but I'm damned if I'll gamble Beth's. The way you're crowding her, you'll push her into tight clothes and back seats before the year is out. She's becoming a woman, Linc. She wants to be beautiful for her man. It's as simple and natural as breathing. If you try to make her hold her breath, you'll have a backlash that could ruin her life. She is a good, bright, loving person. Show her how to be the kind of woman a man can trust with his love."

"I'm trying to," he said evenly.

"By keeping her in pigtails?"

"By keeping her from turning out like her mother."

"Haven't you been listening? *Beth is not like her mother.*"

"Then why are you trying to make her look like she is?" retorted Linc. "Any man worth the name can look past Beth's outside."

"Assuming that he sees her in the first place."

"What?"

"How many good, kind, *plain* women have you given a second look to?" she asked sweetly.

Linc said nothing.

Holly laughed sarcastically. "Then there's Cyn. She wears enough paint for a barn. Why is it all right for her to be beautiful and all wrong for Beth or me?"

"Cyn can wear paint and tight clothes and rub all over men because she's a . . . toy. No grown man will fall in love with a toy, no matter how perfectly it's wrapped. So," he smiled narrowly, "why not enjoy the wrappings?"

"I see your point," murmured Holly. "Having a plain wife would be so boring you'd need to unwrap some fancy toys from time to time."

"That's not what I meant!" Linc crossed the room and put his hands on Holly's arms as though he was afraid she, too, would run away. "You aren't plain, Holly."

"I know that," she said calmly. "But do you? Do you really believe that I'm as beautifully wrapped as Cyn?"

"You don't have to be," he said roughly. "Wives have enough power over their husbands without that." He put his hand on her abdomen in a gesture that was both possessive and gentle. "What do you think it does to a man to know that someday his baby will grow inside the woman he loves? What do you think it does to a man when a woman cares enough to risk her neck dragging him out of a lightning storm? What do you think it does to a man when he goes to sleep with her taste in his mouth and wakes up to her sleepy smile? My God, Holly. Next to those things, beauty is just a cruel joke."

"Physical beauty has nothing to do with those things, Linc. It doesn't make them happen and it doesn't prevent them."

"You're wrong," he said flatly. "I know a lot more about beautiful bitches than you do."

The words *beautiful* and *bitch* don't mean the same thing."

He strode to the dresser, yanked open a drawer and pulled out a framed photo. He handed it to her. "My mother."

The woman in the photograph was extraordinary. She had radiant skin pulled taut over a bone structure that would give her beauty until the day she died. Her hair was thick, long, framing her face in a chestnut cascade. Her eyes were large, set well apart and jade green. Her mouth was wide, invitingly curved, poised on the brink of a smile or a kiss.

"She's the most beautiful woman I've ever seen," said Holly sincerely.

"Yeah." Linc's lips twisted bitterly. "Mother had me five months after she and Dad were married. At the time, he was an agent in Hollywood. She was a model who wanted to be a star." His lips thinned into a grim smile. "There wasn't much call for pregnant models or starlets, so it's obvious I was an accident. I was five weeks old when Dad's father died and left the ranch to him."

Linc ran his hand through his dark hair. "Dad was happy to come here. He hadn't liked being an agent, but he and grandfather had never gotten along. Mother didn't want to come here. My earliest memories are of them yelling about here versus Hollywood." He grimaced. "By the time I was three, mother was back modeling. At least, that's what she called it. I suppose she even wore clothes from time to time.

"Dad didn't buy them, though. Paying off inheritance taxes almost broke him. He kept the ranch, but nothing else. And he worked. My God, how he worked. Dawn to dark and then some."

"It must have been hard for them," said Holly hesitantly.

"Not for her. Not that one. She'd go to Palm Springs. There wasn't any money for baby-sitters so she'd take me along. I don't know how old I was when I realized she wasn't modeling clothes in those motel rooms. After that, I spent a lot of hours locked in cars in the motel parking lots."

Holly's eyes burned with sympathy, but she said nothing. She sensed that if she interrupted him now, he would never speak about it again.

"I was seven when she locked me in the last one." His eyes looked through her, focused on a past that was too painful to remember. "It was hot. I waited and waited for her to come back. I finally fell asleep. When I woke up, it was dark and I was shivering. I waited. No one came. I wanted to get out of that car, but I knew mother would raise welts on me if I did." He shook his head. "It's hard to believe how scared a kid can get. By the time my dad found me the next morning, I was a mess."

Tears welled up and fell silently down Holly's cheeks, but she made no move toward him. She didn't want to hear any more, yet knew she had to. He had kept it inside for too many years, poisoning his own possibilities for love because his father had married the wrong woman.

"I never saw my mother again. She had run off with one of her men. I don't even know if she's still alive. Not that it matters. She never wanted me and I learned to live without her." He shrugged, but his eyes were still focused on the past. "Dad didn't learn much at all. Three years later he married Jan. I don't have a picture of her. I don't need one. Honey blond, slim, turquoise eyes, eighteen when they married. Beautiful? Hell, yes.

"I was fifteen when Beth was born. Jan had been a model in some of the better Palm Springs stores before she got pregnant. When Beth was two months old, Jan went back to modeling. She liked the money that the ranch was finally bringing in, but she didn't like the ranch itself. She ignored Beth. She didn't even like Dad to hold his daughter. All I can figure is that Jan was jealous of her own kid."

Holly looked down at her hands. They ached from being clenched together to keep from touching Linc. She wanted to hold him, to comfort him, to love him. She wanted to wave a magic wand and make the ugly past vanish so that it couldn't throw grotesque shadows over the future.

"I pretty much raised Beth. Jan was too obsessed with her looks to see anything or anyone else, and Dad—" He sighed. "Dad drank a lot by then. I took over more and more of the ranch. Jan spent more and more time in front of the mirror, looking for the first wrinkle, and Dad found the bottom of a lot of bottles. Somewhere along in there Jan started having men on the side. Dad didn't admire her enough, I guess. I sure as hell didn't admire her as much as she wanted."

Holly made a small sound, but he didn't hear. His face was utterly cold, rigid with contempt.

"She was a real bitch," he said matter-of-factly. "When she couldn't get Dad and me to fight over her, she started bragging about her men. One night she picked up the wrong man. He slapped her around, she called Dad and he went to get her. On the way back home, Dad lost control of the car on a bad curve." For the first time, Linc's eyes focused on Holly. "Your parents were killed because my stepmother couldn't stay in her own bed. If she hadn't died in that crash, I'd have killed her myself. She wasn't worth one tear on your face, *niña*. Not then, not now."

"I'm not crying for her," whispered Holly. Blindly, she went to him, buried her face against his chest and held on with a strength that surprised both of them. "Tomorrow," she said in a strained voice, "tomorrow please don't hold them against me. You aren't your father, Linc. You're strong. He wasn't. I'm not like your mother or stepmother. You have to believe that. Even when you see me tomorrow, you have to believe that."

"Of course I'll believe it," he said, moving his mouth gently over hers, tasting her tears.

"No, you won't," she said in a despairing voice, feeling empty and afraid. "Oh, Linc, you don't know how beautiful I am."

The phone rang, startling in the silence. Slowly he let go of Holly and answered the phone. Holly heard a voice inform him that the mare was down again. He hung up and started for the door. Once in the hall, he hesitated as though he wanted to say more. Then he turned and was gone.

For a long time Holly stood motionless, tears running down her face, afraid of the midnight to come.

7

·000000000·

Holly, are you awake?"

Beth's voice brought Holly out of a restless sleep. She rolled over in the huge bed and kicked off the comforter she didn't remember pulling over herself. "I'm awake."

"Can I come in?"

"Sure," she said, rubbing her neck. She felt awful. Her clothes were wrinkled and awry. She had fallen asleep while waiting for Linc to come back from the barn. But he hadn't come back.

Beth walked in, carrying a cordless phone. She stopped. "Are you awake enough to talk to your boss?" she asked doubtfully.

Holly stretched, then rolled her head, trying to relieve the tension in her neck muscles. "Sure, why not?" she said in a tired voice. She reached for the phone.

Beth put it on the bed and turned to leave.

"Stick around," said Holly. "I may need first aid when he's finished." She smiled, but her voice was serious. She knew that Roger would not be happy when he found out where she was staying. Camping alone was one thing. Living with a man was something else entirely. And yesterday she had left a note at the hotel telling Roger that she could be reached at the home of Lincoln McKenzie. She had also explained that until further notice, Roger was to call her Holly.

Beth's eyes widened. "Are you supposed to be working?"

"No. It's just that Roger won't be happy to know I'm with Linc."

"Is Roger your boyfriend?"

Holly shook her head. "He thought he wanted to be. He really doesn't, but I sometimes have a hard time convincing him."

"Will he fire you?"

Smiling, Holly reached for the phone. "I doubt it. I'm too good at what I do. He'll just be touchy for a while." She flipped the switch that activated the receiver and the speaker. Beth would be able to hear Roger as clearly as she could. "Hi, Roger. You're up early."

"It's ten o'clock in Manhattan. I've been on the phone with Sandra since six," said Roger. "How was the camping trip?"

"Wet, stormy and thoroughly wonderful."

There was a distinct pause. "Is the name Lincoln McKenzie familiar to me?"

"He manages Hidden Springs," said Holly, yawning. "Remember?"

"I remember you saying that there was nothing between you and that hard-eyed cowboy."

Beth smothered her giggle behind her hand, guessing that Linc was the cowboy in question. Holly winked at her.

"I didn't think there was."

"And there is now?"

"Yes."

There was a long silence. Then, softly, "Is he good for you?"

Sudden tears tightened Holly's throat. Roger was

worried about her rather than angry with her. He might want her, but he was also her friend. "I've loved Linc since I was nine," she said. "We were separated when my parents died and Sandra brought me to New York."

"First love. Bloody hell." He laughed shortly. "Who can compete with that?" He hesitated. "Are you sure, Holly? Frankly, he looked like a pretty hard piece of business to me."

"I'm sure."

"Well," he sighed, "as long as you still model for me, I'll try to be a good sport."

"Roger, I'd model for you even if I didn't have a contract. Not only do I like you, but you also create the most incredible clothes in the world. It's exciting just to be around them."

"Thank God. It's too late to replace you, Shan— Holly."

"I'd kill the model who tried," she said.

Roger laughed, pleased. "When you get tired of living with the devil, there's a fair-haired angel who will be glad to lick your wounds."

"Linc isn't a devil."

"From what I saw a few days ago, he'll do until Old Nick comes along," said Roger dryly. "But I didn't call to argue about McKenzie's devilish looks. I'm putting off the Hidden Springs shoot for now. We'll go to Cabo San Lucas instead. The weatherman assures me it's hot, dry and sandy there."

"As opposed to hot, *wet* and sandy here?" said Holly with a lightness she didn't feel. She loved her work, but she didn't want to leave Linc. "How much time before we leave and how long are we staying?"

"We'll leave sometime in the next week. I can't be more specific, because I'm having trouble choosing the male model."

"What happened to the last pretty face?" asked Holly, forgetting everything about the man but his wonderful gray eyes.

"He broke his wrist climbing rocks for a cigarette ad. I'm going to look at a few more models today, and if I don't see anything I like, I'll try something new."

"Roger, no more dumb jocks, please. Smart ones, yes."

"Where's your sense of adventure? That piece of beefcake you're referring to sold a lot of jogging clothes."

"He also kept tackling me," she said acidly.

"So his eyesight was better than his IQ."

"Have you thought of using Linc?" asked Holly, only half joking.

"Love must be blind. Lincoln Mckenzie looks like your desert mountains. Tall, hard and definitely not for the uninitiated. I'd like to think my products are a bit more civilized."

Beth was caught between indignation and laughter. Laughter won. She buried her face in a pillow.

"What's that?" asked Roger. "Sounds like you're choking on toast."

Holly laughed. "That is Linc's younger sister. She thinks he can look pretty rough, too, but that's only when he's mad. The rest of the time he's a pussycat."

"Felis leo, no doubt," said Roger dryly. "I've seen his kind in Africa."

Holly groaned and gave up. "At least come to the party we're having tonight."

"Damn," he said, meaning it. "I don't think I can. Mrs. L'Acara—remember her, the Queen of Diamonds? —called and invited me and the models to come to some rodeo or something. A horse auction, cookout and black-tie ball is how she described it. Naturally I accepted. It sounded terribly improbable and completely western."

"It also sounds like I'll be seeing you in a few hours."

Beth nodded and whispered, "Mrs. L'Acara called yesterday and made arrangements for five more."

"What's that?" asked Roger.

"Mrs. L'Acara is bringing you to the McKenzies' Arabian Nights gala," explained Holly.

"Speak of the devil," murmured Roger. "Well, I'll polish my best set of horns and give the old boy his due."

"Roger—"

"Sorry, love. That's my limit on sour grapes."

"I hope so."

"Save a dance for me, beautiful lady."

He hung up before she could answer.

"He really likes you, doesn't he?" asked Beth.

"He's a friend. No more," Holly smiled, "and no less. You'll like him, Beth. And I know he'll like you."

"Why?"

"Roger always likes beautiful women." Holly yawned again. "What's on the agenda for the morning?"

"Linc's still with the mare. She keeps starting labor and then stopping. Mrs. Malley called last night. Her sister is in intensive care. I told her to stay in Palm Springs." She looked at Holly, worried. "That's all right, isn't it? We can handle the party without the housekeeper, can't we?"

"Looks like we get the chance to try," said Holly, smiling.

She soon lost her smile. Workmen were swarming over the ballroom-sized platform that had been erected previously in the McKenzies' parklike backyard. The men were setting up an enormous black, red and silver tent; evening rain had been forecast again. Out beyond the pool's extensive decks and plantings, two barbecue pits had been dug. A side of beef and a whole pig were cooking slowly. The bartender had set up his station on the side patio amid tubs of fragrant flowers. Although the auction didn't begin until one o'clock, people had been arriving since nine. For the most part they stayed in the sales barn, checking out the horses. Inevitably, some people were more interested in visiting than in buying horses.

By noon, Holly was frustrated and impatient. She had done what she could—soothed caterers, smiled at unwanted guests, lifeguarded at the pool for two children whose mother couldn't say no—she had done everything but see Linc. Every time she started for the foaling barn, a workman grabbed her and started asking where to put this and what to do with that.

By three o'clock, she was determined to get to the barn no matter who stopped her. She wasn't even out of the backyard when a hand grabbed her arm. She turned quickly, not bothering to hide the anger she felt.

"Can't it wait?" she snapped. Then she saw it was Beth. "Sorry. I've been trying to see Linc since nine."

"That's why I'm here. He called from the barn. Dawn Dancer finally came through. She had a filly. Mother and daughter are doing fine."

"Good." She hesitated. "How did Linc sound?"

"Tired," said Beth. "He apologized for losing his temper last night. I apologized, too. But—"

"But?" encouraged Holly.

"It doesn't change how either one of us feels, does it? I mean, I still want to look older than ten and he still wants me to look like a kid. It isn't fair."

"Not much is," said Holly. "Give him time, Beth. He needs to learn that beauty isn't beastly."

Beth looked stubborn. "Does that mean you won't do my hair or makeup for the dance?"

"Of course not. Eight o'clock, as agreed."

Beth held out her hand. "Shake."

Holly took the girl's hand firmly. "Partners in crime."

"What crime?" asked a deep voice behind her.

Holly turned and smiled wryly at Linc. "Don't ask unless you want to suspend the truce again."

"I didn't want to suspend it last night." He rubbed his

hand through his hair tiredly. "I'm sure as hell not up to a battle now."

She stood on tiptoe and kissed him gently on the lips. "Truce, then. I'm not feeling very feisty myself."

He pulled her closer. "That's what happens when you sleep alone," he said too softly for Beth to over-hear.

The caterer called out to Holly and crossed the lawn toward her with determined strides. Holly groaned.

"I'll take care of it," said Beth, heading for the man.

"He's probably complaining about the kitchen again," warned Holly.

"I know. If he needed two microwaves, he should have brought one of his own," muttered Beth.

Linc grabbed Holly's hand and pulled her toward the house. Together, they tiptoed through the kitchen and up the stairs, avoiding guests and workmen alike. When they reached his bedroom, he put the cordless phone out in the hall and shut the door. Then he stretched, flexing his back and arms. Slowly he began to unbutton his shirt. He winced as he shrugged out of the long sleeves.

"Are you still sore?" asked Holly, thinking of the scrapes on his back.

"Just stiff. She was going to have that foal standing up or know the reason why." He smiled wryly and flexed his back again. "She had it lying down, finally. After a while, she got the hang of it and I could let go."

"What you need is a rubdown," said Holly, walking past him toward the bathroom. She came back with the bottle of scented oil she used after her bath. "You'll have to shower afterward," she smiled, "but for now you can just hold your nose."

He inhaled. "Smells fresh, clean. Like you."

With a muffled sigh, he lay facedown in the middle of the bed. The only way Holly could reach him was to get on the bed and put a knee on either side of his hips, straddling him like a horse. She moved into place unself-consciously, warmed some oil in her hands and began to knead the long, resilient muscles of his back, working from the waist upward.

Linc groaned appreciatively. "Who taught you how to do that?"

"My ballet teacher. We were always pulling muscles or straining something, so he taught us how to rub out the kinks."

She worked in silence for a few minutes, admiring the line of his back. His spine was a valley just wide and deep enough to accept her fingertip; on either side rose ridges of muscle. He was built like a professional swimmer, with long, smooth muscles that were as supple as they were powerful. She leaned on her hands, using her weight as leverage to loosen muscles knotted by strain. He groaned, but it wasn't a complaint. Smiling, she warmed more oil and eased forward to knead his shoulders and arms right down to his fingertips.

She massaged him until her hands and wrists ached, but she didn't really notice. There was a pure sensual pleasure in touching him that was almost hypnotic. Until Linc, she had never thought of a man as beautiful, yet there was no other way she could describe him except in terms of beauty. Long after his muscles had relaxed beneath her hands, she continued stroking him. Finally she sighed, flexed her fingers and began working on his legs. After a few moments she made an exasperated sound. The thick fabric of the jeans not only felt unpleasant, it prevented her from following the line of his muscles to work out the knots.

"Are you asleep?" she whispered.

His back shook with silent laughter. "Not likely, niña."

"Any time your back is that tight, so are your legs," she said, sliding off him and standing up. "The jeans have to go."

Linc rolled onto his side. He propped his head on his fist and looked at her. "If I take off my pants, it won't be to get my legs rubbed."

"Sure it will." She smiled. "Trust me."

He rolled onto his back and stretched, watching her out of narrowed hazel eyes. Then his arms shot out. Before she realized what was happening, she was lifted off her feet and pulled over him like a blanket. His legs wrapped around her ankles, imprisoning her. She felt the heat and unmistakable hardness of his arousal.

"It's me I don't trust," he said. His tongue searched her mouth, traced the delicate serrations of her teeth, probed the soft interior of her lips. He made a sound deep in his throat and pulled his mouth away. "You taste better each time."

The ache that had never left her changed suddenly into a lightning stroke of desire. As she shuddered, her hips moved over him in an instinctive, sensuous caress. She lowered her mouth to his, tasting him with slow, thorough strokes. His hands slid beneath her blouse until the tips of her breasts were caught between his fingers. She twisted against him, crying out with need and pleasure.

His hands moved down her back, fitting her against him. Then his strong fingers cupped her hips, rocking her, turning her whole body into one long caress over him. Desire raced through her, an explosion of sensations that made her dig her nails into his arms out of sheer frustration. She wanted his hands to touch her everywhere, his mouth to know her hidden places, his body to become part of her. She wanted to sink into him like rain into the desert, permeating him until there was no Linc, no Holly, only a net of lightning and ecstasy surrounding them.

When he rolled aside, she could have wept in frustration. For a moment there was only the harsh sound of their breathing. His eyes were closed, his muscles rigid along his jaws, his hands clenched.

"Don't you want me, Linc?" she asked raggedly, her voice caught between tears and desire.

With a savage motion, he took her hand and pressed it against his body. Beneath her palm, the outline of his desire was startlingly clear. "What do you think?"

"Then why did you stop?"

He opened eyes that were more green than brown, burning with barely leashed need. "I want your first time to be perfect," he said slowly. He drew a long, uneven breath. "I don't want to make love to you with one ear on the door, waiting for some fool guest to barge in. I don't want to love you just once and then have to get out of bed and be host to a hundred people." His lips twisted into a wry smile. "And I for damn sure don't want to smell like the bottom of the barn."

"You smell like Romance to me," she said, nuzzling his chest.

He lifted his eyebrow in silent query.

She smiled and pointed to the bottle of scented oil on the bedside table. " 'Romance.' "

"Only the top half of me smells good," he said, rolling out of bed in a single motion. "The jeans could stand up and walk without me."

"Have you heard of that modern convenience called a shower?" she asked. "And another one called a lock?" She got up and walked to the door that connected the bedroom with the office. She slid the bolt home. Without looking at him, she walked to the hall door. The bolt clicked into place. She turned with all of her model's grace and walked toward him. At each step, her fingers undid another button of her blouse. "Now, about that shower."

For an instant she thought he was going to agree— and so did he. Then he stepped into the bathroom and locked the door behind him. She leaned against the door, letting the cool wood soothe her flushed body.

"Linc?" she whispered, knowing he couldn't hear unless he, too, was leaning against the door.

He was.

"I have to show horses on the auction block in ten minutes. If that's enough time for you"—the lock clicked open—"then come in."

"You're the expert," she said. "Is that enough time?"

"For some women, it's nine minutes more than I'd care to spend. For you, I'd want at least a lifetime."

"Starting when?" she groaned. "Damn it, Linc, you're not being fair!"

He laughed softly. "You're not the only one who's hurting, *niña*. I'll make it up to you tonight. To both of us. Deal?"

Holly thought of several things to say, none of which were approved for ladies. She set her teeth and pushed away from the door. "Deal."

She buttoned her blouse and went to find the caterer. If the man still wanted to argue about microwaves, she was ready.

Beth fidgeted, unable to contain her excitement. "Can I look yet?"

Smiling, Holly unwrapped a long strand of blond hair from a fat roller. "Not yet."

"What are you doing?"

"Brushing the hair that I didn't braid."

"I'm so excited," whispered Beth.

"Really?" teased Holly. "I'd never have guessed it."

"You're as bad as Linc." Beth grimaced and tried to sit still. "I saw Jack."

"Which one was he?" said Holly, trying to remember one face out of the group of teen-agers who had arrived just in time for the barbecue.

"The good-looking one."

"They all looked pretty good to me."

Beth giggled. "He was standing next to the little redhead. She's my best friend."

"Oh, *that* good-looking one." Holly untied the cloth she had used to protect Beth's clothes. "Okay. Stand up and be counted."

With a subdued squeal, Beth leaped up and hurried toward the mirrored sliding doors that covered Linc's closet.

"Oh. . . ." Beth's eyes widened as she looked at her own image. Hair the color of late-afternoon sunlight fanned over the silk of her blouse, curled over the gentle swell of her young breasts. The turquoise skirt fell in graceful folds from her slim waist to the tips of her silver sandals. Tiny drop earrings glowed like an echo of her turquoise eyes. "I'm pretty!"

"You're more than that, Beth," said Holly, smoothing a last lock of blond hair. "You're beautiful."

A shadow passed over her young face. "I look like my mother," she said, her voice suddenly empty. "Was she—" Beth hesitated, then finished in a rush, as though if she spoke quickly it wouldn't hurt so much. "Was she really a—a bad woman?"

Holly couldn't lie and did not want to tell the truth. "Your mother was a very unhappy woman," she said finally. "Unhappy women do unhappy things."

For a moment Beth looked much older than her fifteen years. "And I look like her."

"That's just the outside," said Holly in a firm voice. She hugged the girl and added fiercely, "You're a good person, Beth McKenzie. Whatever your mother was or wasn't has nothing to do with you today."

"Linc doesn't seem to believe that," said Beth uncertainly.

"Two beautiful women hurt him very badly. So I guess it will take two other beautiful women to teach him that beauty and cruelty aren't synonyms." She tipped Beth's face up and studied the girl's clear eyes. "Will you help me teach him?"

Beth nodded slowly.

"Good. Now, I've got to do my caterpillar-to-butterfly act. Wait for me?"

"Sure. Can I help?"

"Nope. I want to surprise you, too."

Holly closed the bathroom door behind her. She had showered and set her hair earlier. All that remained was to put on her dress and makeup, and comb out her hair. She took the long black dress off its hanger. As always, the dress delighted her. Its lines were simple and elegant. The neckline was a wide, shallow curve that stretched from shoulder to shoulder. The bodice fitted her like a shadow of her own beauty. There was no back, simply a black fall of silk from waist to ankle. The skirt swung enticingly with each movement of her body.

Inset at the bottom of each short sleeve was an inverted V strung with loops of unbelievably fine gold chain. The chains were repeated in a diamond shape between her breasts. The gold warmed against her skin, shifting and gleaming with each breath she took. Although very little of her was revealed through the closely spaced chains, they hung in loops that tempted a man's finger into searching beneath the sensual glow of eighteen-carat gold.

She smoothed the dress into place, then put on a cover-up that went from chin to ankles. She opened her cosmetic case. Smiling, she went to work. Foundation so sheer it was all but invisible. Blusher that heightened the slanting line of her cheekbones. A touch of scented oil smoothed into each black eyebrow. Shadow to bring out the tawny color of her eyes. Liner applied artfully, all but hidden, transforming tilted eyes into cat eyes, unblinking and gold. Mascara touched on lashes that were unreasonably long. A smooth, tawny-rose lip gloss that emphasized the sensuality of her mouth.

With practiced motions, she stripped the rollers out of her hair. She brushed with long strokes that made her hair crackle and shift as though it were alive, restless, wild to be free. She caught up some of the hair at the sides, making silky wings that covered half of her ears, then clipped it in place at the back of her head. Her clip was a twist of gold capped by a long tassel of chains that matched those on her dress. Except for that single restraint, she allowed her hair to fall down her bare back until hair and silk were indistinguishable.

She slipped into high-heeled gold sandals, removed the wrap that had protected her dress, examined herself critically in the mirror—and froze. Never had her transformation been so startling, so complete. The sensual awakening that Linc had begun showed in the heat of her skin, the catlike shine of her eyes, the bruised impatience of her mouth. With a mixture of pride and fear, she realized that she had never looked more alluring.

She opened the bathroom door. Beth didn't hear. She was standing in front of the television, staring at the screen with a peculiarly intent look. Holly heard the words before she saw the picture: *". . . Royce, made to be worn over nothing more than a woman's perfumed skin."* It was a commercial she had made last year, featuring a line of lingerie that had since sold very well.

"Beth?"

"I've seen that commercial a hundred times," said Beth without turning around. "She has to be the most gorgeous woman in the world."

"Thank you."

Startled, Beth turned and saw Holly for the first time. "Holly . . . ?" she said weakly.

"The same," said Holly, smiling. "Well, almost the same. A Royce does wonders for any woman, and Roger designed this dress especially for me."

"I—I—" Beth swallowed and tried again. "I can't believe it," she said finally. "Why didn't you tell us?"

"I said I was a model. I am. What was I supposed to

say?" she asked dryly. " 'Hi, I'm Shannon, the internationally famous model.' If you're famous, you don't
have to mention it, do you?"

Beth shook her head. Then she started laughing.
"Wait until Cyn sees you! Oh, I want to be there. I want
to be right *there!*"

"Thought you might," said Holly. "That's why I
asked you to wait."

"And Linc. Oh boy, when Linc sees—" Beth stopped
abruptly, realizing that Linc was not going to be delighted. "God, Holly. He's going to have a fit."

"Yeah," she said, trying to smile. "That's the other
reason I wanted you to wait. I don't think he'll kill me in
front of his kid sister." She took a deep breath, settled
her Shannon persona firmly into place and held out her
hand to Beth. "First things first. Let's go see how far
Cyn's jaw can drop."

8

It was very dark by the time Holly and Beth stepped outside. Flying clouds hid all but occasional pale flashes of moon. Hundreds of strings of tiny white lights wove through trees and over fences, guiding people to the dance pavilion. Music rippled through the night, strains of a waltz that was centuries old. The pavilion was just beginning to fill, drawing laughter and beautifully dressed couples into its billowing interior.

Some people had attended the auction and barbecue and then gone to their nearby homes to change into evening clothes. Others had brought their formal clothes and changed in one of the McKenzies' six guest rooms. Still others had simply attended the auction looking as princely as the Arabians they had come to admire and buy. The mixture of fashion and silk-tasseled horses gave Holly a feeling of being transported to a fairy-tale world where gleaming Arabians danced amid a diamond glitter of wealth.

"What a stunning animal," breathed Holly, looking

across the yard to the auction platform. A dark stallion pranced with muscular elegance at the end of a braided-silk show halter. With each movement, elaborate silk tassels rippled, weaving light into beautiful patterns.

"That's Night Dancer," said Beth, following Holly's glance.

"Surely you aren't selling him!"

Beth laughed. "No, just showing off the best Arabian stud this side of anywhere. Linc does it at the end of every auction."

Holly waited for a few moments more, watching the spotlighted platform. But it was not the stallion her eyes sought out, it was the tall man in the shadows who held the horse's silken lead. From this distance she could not discern any features; only the man's potent grace as he controlled Night Dancer identified him as Linc.

"He's quite an animal, isn't he?" asked Beth.

"Yes." Holly smiled and added dryly, "Both of them."

Giggling, Beth picked up her long skirt and began walking toward the pavilion. Holly followed, holding folds of smooth midnight silk in her hands. Linc didn't see them. He was already heading back to the barn, leading the ranch's most valuable asset.

Holly and Beth joined the glittering guests inside the pavilion. The bandstand was at one end of the enclosure, a bar and buffet at the other, with groupings of tables and chairs in between.

"There's Cyanide," said Beth, taking Holly's arm and leading her toward the left.

"Cyanide?" Holly glanced beyond Beth. Across the room, flanked by several men, was a petite blonde in a long, tight red sheath that was slit to mid-thigh in front. "Oh, you mean Cyn."

Beth tugged at Holly's arm impatiently. "Let's go."

"Give her a minute or two. I hate to spoil her evening right off."

"Why? She's spoiled enough of mine. Come on."

Holly smiled. "Slow down, Beth. Let me do it my way."

Beth gave a longing glance to the spot where Cyn stood in sequin-studded splendor, radiating the kind of signals guaranteed to bring every male within reach to attention. "What's your way?" she sighed finally.

"Stay with me. Introduce me to everyone you know. There's more to attracting men—and *keeping* them attracted—than a flashy red dress."

"After I've introduced you, what then?"

"Then I'll cut off her claws and make a bracelet for you."

Something in Holly's voice made Beth look at her closely. "You know," said Beth, "I hope you don't ever get mad at me."

"I only get mad at people who are cruel." Holly smiled, softening her expression. "Come on. I've got a roomful of people to meet."

" 'People?' Not just men?"

" 'People,' " Holly repeated firmly.

"Where should we start?"

"Do you know the gray-haired gentleman and the woman in the lavender dress?"

"Sure. But he's old."

Holly's lips quirked. "Button, no man is *that* old."

Beth gave her a I-hope-you-know-what-you're-doing look, took her hand and led her to the couple. "Hi, George, Mary. This is Holly North, Linc's—"

"I'm a friend of the family," said Holly quickly, before Beth could say "fiancée." After tonight, she wasn't sure that Linc would want to see her again, much less marry her. But she wouldn't think about that now. She held out her hand to the man and then his wife. It was not the first time she had hidden sorrow behind a breathtaking smile. "I'm delighted to meet you, Mr.—?"

"Johnston," said the man, taking her hand. "But call me George."

"Only if you call me Holly," she said, squeezing his hand gently. She released his hand and turned toward his wife. "That's a lovely color on you, Mrs. Johnston. I envy you. If I wear lavender, I look like I have terminal flu." The compliment was genuine, for Holly disliked even the social lies that she had learned were sometimes necessary.

"Please, call me Mary." The woman's shrewd blue eyes weighed Holly, then forgave her for being too beautiful. She smiled. "The idea of you being jealous of me is almost funny."

"Not to me," said Holly ruefully. "I love purples and can't wear any of them."

"George and Mary own a ranch about three miles up the valley," said Beth. "They raise quarter horses."

Holly gave George a sideways look. "You'll be disowned if you're caught at an Arabian auction."

George and Mary both laughed. "Actually," he admitted, "my favorite riding horse is half Arab."

That began an enthusiastic discussion of various equine breeds and crossbreeds. George and Mary leaped into the conversation; their lives, like those of many people in Garner Valley, revolved around horses. Soon, other people joined the conversation, drawn by the laughter and the charming, beautiful woman who was at its center.

As Holly was introduced to new people, she memorized names and faces. She complimented each person, always honestly, and guided the conversation so that no one was left out. When the group became too large for easy conversation, she signaled Beth with a glance and withdrew without leaving a ripple behind.

Beth looked bemused. "What now?" she whispered.

"More people." Holly winked at her. "Don't look so disappointed. I like meeting people."

"I don't see how married couples are going to make Cyn eat her words," said Beth bluntly.

"Watch," smiled Holly. She looked at a young

couple standing alone and rather uncertainly at the edge of the dance floor. "Do you know them?"

Beth sighed and led Holly over toward the couple. Within a few minutes, other young couples were drawn like bright leaves into a whirlpool. Then several men and women who were alone joined in. The conversation ranged from horses to politics to the intricacies of downhill skiing. Again, Holly became the center of an animated, laughing group. Again, it was her real interest in people rather than her beauty alone that held their attention. Again, Holly withdrew unobtrusively.

As Beth led Holly toward another area of the room, the younger girl whispered, "I'm catching on. At least two of those men left Cyn to join our group."

Holly made a noncommittal sound and looked around the room. Linc wasn't there. She had hoped he would come, see her making friends and maybe not be so angry with her Shannon appearance. With her luck, he wouldn't get here until she went to work peeling the handsome singles off Cyn. She grimaced. She enjoyed meeting people. She did not enjoy playing Mata Hari. But in her job as the Royce Reflection, she had learned to do both.

She had gathered and faded out of two more groups, but Linc still hadn't arrived. It became impossible to find new people to meet, because she couldn't move ten feet without being asked to dance. Her campaign to charm the people who lived and worked with Linc was an unqualified success, one that she enjoyed as much as the people who warmed themselves in her presence. But Linc had seen none of it.

"Well," she murmured to Beth, "let's get it over with."

Beth and Holly walked toward Cyn. It took ten minutes to go fifty feet because Holly was graciously refusing offers of food or dance or conversation at every step.

"Okay, Beth. I want you to distract her. I'll come in

from the back. And"—she smiled gently—"why don't you help me? Two of the men don't look much older than you."

Beth looked startled.

"Don't you know them?" asked Holly.

"Yes, but—"

Holly waited.

"What do you want me to do?" asked Beth.

"Do you like any of the men?"

"Oh, sure. Jim's a lot of fun, and even though he's only nineteen, he's the best trainer in the valley, next to Linc."

"Then tell him."

Beth blinked and nibbled on her lower lip.

"Go ahead," encouraged Holly. "Nobody will bite you for being honest. Except Cyn, of course. Don't be honest with her. Ignore her."

Holly watched while Beth walked slowly toward Cyn. When the girl was only a few feet away, her chin came up and her posture straightened. As Holly moved to circle around, she saw Cyn's look of surprise and heard her clearly.

"Well, well, since when does Linc let you play dress up?"

Holly held her breath and hoped that Beth would hold her tongue. Beth turned and smiled at the young man next to Cyn. Holly couldn't hear what was said, but it was clear that the young man's attention was no longer on Cyn.

"Where's your chum?" said Cyn. "The plain one, little miss what's-her-name."

Beth looked up and smiled. "Right behind you, Cyanide."

Cyn turned and looked past Holly, not recognizing her. Then Cyn looked again. Her mouth opened and closed and opened once more.

"Hello, Cyn," said Holly. She turned her brightest smile on the stranger who had his right hand posses-

sively on Cyn's arm. "I'm sure I would have remembered if we had been introduced," murmured Holly,
holding out her hand. "I'm Holly."

He gave Holly the kind of up-and-down look that she
found distasteful, but she kept her smile in place.

"I'm Stan," he said, taking her hand in both of his
and drawing her closer. "Where on earth did you come
from? Or was it heaven?"

"Manhattan," she said, hoping no one would notice
her thinning smile. She looked at the other, older man
from beneath long black lashes. As her right hand was
securely held, she offered her left. "And you?"

"Gary. I'm just along for the ride," he said dryly,
taking her hand.

Holly looked at him more closely, then gave him a
genuine smile. "Aren't we all?" she murmured.

Gary reassessed her in a single glance, smiled and
nodded. He tucked her hand under his arm. "You look
thirsty," he said, and began to lead her away.

"Not so fast, buddy," protested Stan, refusing to let
go of her hand.

Holly glanced over her shoulder just in time to see
Beth quietly leading Jim and the other young man
toward the buffet. Cyn didn't notice. She was still
staring at Holly in total disbelief. Holly smiled gently at
her before turning to Stan. "I'm sure there's more than
one glass of champagne at the bar. Why don't you join
us?"

He didn't have to be asked twice. Less than three
minutes after Holly had said hello, Cyn was left standing alone.

By the time Holly disengaged from the disappointed
men, Roger, Jerry and three models had arrived.
Roger's immaculate good looks attracted as many
women's glances as Holly attracted men's. When they
danced together, people stared; the combination of light
and dark was arresting. As always, Holly enjoyed

Roger's easy wit and conversation, but her eyes kept searching the pavilion for Linc.

"Missing someone?" asked Roger, his tone playful and his blue eyes intent.

"Mmm," said Holly absently. She noticed that Cyn had collected another group of men. "Excuse me. I have some claws to trim."

"Will you be long?"

Holly's lips curved. "Five minutes. Ten at most. Why don't you make some women happy and dance with them?"

Holly walked quickly toward Cyn. A few minutes later Holly walked away, followed by several men. The scene repeated itself, with variations in the cast of men, several more times in the next hour and a half. Only two things didn't change—Roger's presence and Holly's anxiety about Linc. Roger watched with increasing perplexity and amusement while she repeatedly stripped Cyn of admirers and herded them to the other end of the room.

"Why do I get the feeling you have something against the little blonde with the big . . . sequins?" asked Roger, laughter rippling beneath his words.

"What?" said Holly, trying to look for Linc without being obvious about it. She was sure that she had sensed his presence, but each time she looked she couldn't find him. Then she realized what Roger had said. She smiled with some bitterness. "Yes, I suppose you could say that."

"Competition for the cowboy?" he asked lightly.

She looked around the pavilion once more before answering. A sense of Linc's presence kept shivering across her nerves, telling her that he was nearby, but she couldn't find him in the brightly lit tent. She looked over her shoulder, but saw only darkness outside. No one was on the lighted walkway leading to the pavilion. She turned back to Roger. "It's a long story."

One corner of his mouth turned up. "Perfectly all right. It'll be ten or fifteen minutes before Cyn collects enough men to make it worth the walk." He looked over Holly's shoulder and smiled cynically. "Guess she finally figured it out."

Holly turned and saw Cyn leaving the pavilion on Jerry's arm.

"Want to make a last foray?" offered Roger.

"Wouldn't dream of it. They deserve each other."

Roger waited.

Holly's smile widened. Of all the people she knew, Roger was the most likely to enjoy the story of Cyn's discomfort. Overdressed blondes irritated his sense of proportion.

"Cyn and Beth—that's Linc's younger sister—don't like each other. Cyn called Beth a plain little thing. Beth believed her. When I told Beth she wasn't plain, Cyn asked what I could know about it, since I was as plain as a concrete slab." Holly smiled slightly as Roger's jaw sagged in disbelief. "The upshot of it was that I bet Cyn I could have men standing in line to talk to me at this dance . . ."

Roger laughed and laughed. "She called you plain?" he said incredulously. "I suspected she wasn't very smart, but I didn't know she was blind." —

Holly's smile was as brilliant as her eyes. "I do look a bit different when I'm not dressed up."

"That," said Linc's cold voice behind her, "is the understatement of the century."

Roger looked from Holly's stricken face to Linc's narrow-eyed fury. Despite Linc's obvious anger, he was handsome enough to break her heart. His evening clothes had been tailored to fit the long, lean lines of his body. Every time he moved, the material outlined another aspect of his masculine grace and power.

Roger looked at the two of them, so consumed by each other that no one else existed, yet Linc's anger was

as real and potentially dangerous as lightning. With a
soft curse, Roger put a finger under Holly's chin, turning
her head until she was looking at him rather than Linc.
"I don't know why he's mad, but instinct tells me that
his bite is worse than any bark I've ever heard. If you
need first aid, you know my room number. Hear me,
Shannon?"

She nodded.

He gave Linc an unreadable look. "If she comes to
me, you're a bloody idiot. I'll wrap her in silk bandages
and you'll never see her again." He stared back into her
eyes, tilted, mysterious, almost afraid. "Some men are
as dangerous as they look. Be careful, love." He kissed
her lips lightly, brushed past Linc and disappeared into
the darkness beyond the pavilion.

Linc made a bitter sound. "It's a wonder that he isn't
immune to pretty faces." He looked her over with a
thoroughness that made her weak. His eyes lingered on
the fine chains that dipped and quivered between her
breasts. "Before I even got out of the house, people
were coming up to me and telling me what a charmer
Beth's friend Holly North was. Not just the men, but the
women, too. So I hurried out here to enjoy you—and I
couldn't find you. I found someone else, though.
What's that name again? Shannon?"

"Yes," she said nervously. Then, more clearly, "Yes,
Shannon. My mother's maiden name. My middle
name. No secret, Linc."

He muttered a single, vicious word. "No secret?
Christ, what kind of a fool do you think I am?" He
heard his own words and laughed with a bitterness that
made her wince. "Scratch that question. You already
know what kind of fool I am." He looked at her with
cold, hungry eyes, the eyes of a predator. "I'm the fool
who thought you were a virgin."

She started to speak, but could only gasp with pain as
his fingers ground against her wrists.

"No," he said coldly. "Not one lying word. See you at midnight, *Shannon.*" He dropped her wrists and strode into the crowd without a backward look.

The rest of the evening moved by in a haze of misery for Holly. Even Beth's transparent glee at Cyn's rout brought only a small smile to Holly's lips. She kept up the facade of charm and pleasure as best she could, but her heart was counting the minutes to midnight. Linc was like the music, present everywhere.

No matter how often she turned around, he was there, watching her the way a cat watches a butterfly just beyond its reach. She could only hope that by midnight he would be willing to listen to her. If she explained that she had been dancing and flirting only to win a bet for Beth, he would understand. If she told him that it was the truce he had insisted on that had kept her silent about the details of her career as Shannon, he would get over his rage. If she told him she loved him— She started as a hand closed on her arm just below the gleaming gold chains.

"It's midnight," said Linc. His voice, like his expression, was remote. He pulled her toward the dance floor with a strength that was just short of bruising. When they were in the center of the floor, he turned her to face him. "Smile, Shannon," he said coldly. "You've smiled at every other damn man tonight, why not me?"

Her lips trembled. "You matter too much to me for easy smiles."

His lips formed a cynical curve. "Very good, Shannon. I'll have to compliment Roger. He's made you a sure winner in the Pleasure Riding class."

The double entendre went through Holly like a knife. Before she could say anything, Linc's arm closed around her. Moving with him because she had no choice, they began dancing to the lyric strains of the same ancient waltz that had begun the evening.

Holly stumbled, finding it impossible to dance because her head was tilted back and held by the pressure of his arm over her long hair. She stumbled again, wincing as her hair jerked against the vise of his arm around her waist. When she reached back with her left hand to free her hair, he pulled her abruptly closer, making her trip and fall against him. She tried to protest, only to have his arm close so ruthlessly around her that she could not breathe at all. When she tried to break free, he simply lifted her feet off the ground.

She had always known he was strong, but had never thought he would use his strength against her like this. He left her just enough breath to keep from fainting, just enough leverage so that her feet did not drag, just enough freedom of movement so that her imprisonment was not obvious. She opened her mouth to speak again, only to gasp as he jerked her against his unyielding body in a casual display of power that forced her to fight for breath.

"Don't say a word." Linc looked down at her with eyes that were dark, glittering with reflected light and anger. "If I hear one more lie out of those pretty lips, I'll—"

His arm kept tightening, squeezing the breath out of her, and the hand holding hers forced bone against bone. Tears magnified her golden eyes. She turned pale, but couldn't even make a sound of pain. He closed his eyes. Abruptly, he loosened his hold. She took a deep breath and cautiously moved her head, trying to ease the unnatural angle of her neck. His arm shifted, freeing her hair.

His hand slid underneath her hair, caressing the bare skin of her back. Hidden by the silky fall of her hair, his fingers probed beneath the open waist of her dress until he could feel the taut curves of her buttocks. With a harsh sound he forced her hips against his. The message of his desire was unmistakable through the thin silk of her dress, yet his face showed nothing but contempt. She struggled to put some distance between them. She succeeded only in rubbing over him in a way that both aroused and embarrassed her.

"No, Linc. Please," she said, pushing futilely against his strength.

"You danced with every other man," he said, his fingers probing intimately beneath her dress, "why not me?"

"I didn't dance like this!"

Air rushed out of her as she was once again yanked against his body. "I said no more lies, Shannon."

"I'm not—"

"Shut up!"

Anger coursed through her like lightning. "It's your party, Linc," she said in a cold voice. "If you want a floor show, I'll give you one."

"Yeah, I bet you do a sensational striptease."

"You lose," she snarled. "A down-and-out brawl was more what I had in mind."

Her voice was loud enough that several other couples looked at them curiously. Linc smiled blandly at her, but suddenly she was off her feet again. She didn't bother flailing about with her feet or telling him he was hurting her. He knew precisely what he was doing. Deliberately, her left hand moved from his shoulder to the still-swollen place where his head had struck a boulder. Her nails brushed lightly over the bruised, sensitive skin. Though she did nothing more, the threat was clear. His expression showed an instant of surprise as he studied her determined face.

"Who taught you to fight dirty?" he asked mildly, returning her feet to the floor.

"You."

Oddly, he smiled. "There are other ways to fight." He shifted his hold on her, giving her freedom to dance. At first she moved stiffly, too angry and wary to allow herself to blend with him. He gathered her against him with a slow, sensual care that mocked her anger.

"You know," he breathed against her ear, "I can't decide which is most silky—your dress, your hair or your skin." His fingertips traced her spine with delicate care, sending showers of sensation over her. He felt her shiver and laughed softly. He brought his left hand in, holding her right against his chest. The back of his hand brushed lightly over her breast each time she breathed. "Not all of you is silky," he murmured. "Some of you gets delightfully hard."

Her breath caught as his knuckle slowly circled the tip of her breast. It was not his hand at her waist that was holding her close to him, but rather her own desire to feel his warmth radiating through the thin silk of her dress. He let go of her fingers and filled his palm with the sweet weight of her breast.

She knew she should protest, but could not. She shook her hair until it fell like a dark curtain around her. She felt his sharp intake of breath as her hair concealed his hand. His groan was a bare thread of sound against her ear. Fingernails rasped lightly over silk, then closed around her nipple.

"Linc . . ." she said in soft protest.

"Shhh," he said. "No one can see." His hand moved toward the warm gold links that filled the diamond between her breasts. His fingers eased between the chains, seeking her warmth. "I've wanted to do this since I walked in and saw you."

For an instant she was shocked by the realization that she was in a roomful of people and his fingers were stroking her naked breasts. Whatever protest she might have made was lost in a sunburst of sensations that radiated from the pit of her stomach. Her back arched against his touch in a reflex as old as passion. She felt the tremor that went through his body, the sudden tension in his muscles that she had come to recognize as heightened desire.

"I want to taste you," he said, holding her tightly, his voice thick. "I want to slide over you like that damn witch's dress and then I want to—"

Abruptly, he released her and led her toward the door.

"What about your guests?" she said.

"I said my good-byes before midnight."

"Beth—"

"Beth left with her girl friend an hour ago. She won't be back until tomorrow."

The night was thick with clouds and the distant rumble of thunder. Raindrops from a recent shower reflected the walkway lights like crystal tears. When Holly stopped to gather the hem of her dress out of the reach of puddles, Linc lifted her into his arms with savage impatience. He walked with long strides toward the house. A fold of silk escaped her fingers, but she couldn't move to gather it up again.

"Linc—"

"No more excuses," he said in a harsh voice. "Beth is gone, the guests know their way home and I'm not going to wait any longer."

Holly looked at his face, outlined in shadows and white light. It was the face of a stranger who knew neither kindness nor love.

"Don't look at me like that," he said impatiently. "Your game of tease and retreat is over, Shannon. Now it's my turn."

9

Linc shut the bedroom door and shot the bolt. He pulled off his tie, tossed it over a chair and unbuttoned his shirt. He unzipped his pants and kicked them aside.

"What are you waiting for?" he said curtly, his hands on the waistband of his underwear. "Take off your clothes." He peeled off his briefs and tossed them aside.

Holly turned her back quickly. She had seen him without clothes in the camp tent, but that had been different, intimate and warm and exciting. This was like watching a stranger undress. Suddenly she felt him behind her. His naked strength pressed against her as his fingers closed possessively over the taut curves of her hips.

"Hurry up," he said in a husky voice, "or I'll take you right here."

Her hands trembled toward the zipper hidden beneath a fold of silk at the back of the dress. Her fingers touched his hardness. She jerked back as though burned.

He swore savagely. "Knock it off, Shannon. You're no more a shivering virgin than I am."

She turned and faced him. "I didn't lie to you. I've never made love with anyone but you." Her voice shook with intensity.

"Yeah, sure."

His hand found the zipper, yanked it down. The dress slid to the floor. She wore nothing beneath but black lace bikinis. He lifted her and pulled off the pants with impatient fingers. His mouth descended, forcing her lips apart. His hands clamped over her hips, lifting her against him with the same careless strength that he had used earlier on the dance floor. The intimate contact surprised her. She didn't know how to respond or what he expected from her. Her earlier arousal gave way to confusion.

"What do you want me to do?" she asked.

He made a disgusted sound, then carried her across the room and dumped her on the bed. Before she could move, she was pinned beneath his weight. His mouth closed over hers, shutting off any protest she might have made. His hands raked over her body, demanding a response that she was too inexperienced to give. His weight and intensity overwhelmed her. After a few minutes she didn't move. He swore and braced himself on his elbows, looking down at her with eyes that had no color, simply darkness.

"It's better if you cooperate," he said.

"I don't know what you want," she said desperately.

"You don't give up, do you? Well, neither do I."

His mouth met hers with a ruthlessness that shocked her. His hands moved between her thighs, forcing her legs apart. She twisted her head aside until she could speak.

"Linc, wait. I'm not ready, Linc," she said, fear and confusion tightening her voice.

"Teases are never ready," he said savagely. "But I am, Shannon. I've been ready since you held your arms out to me in Palm Springs and begged me to do *this.*"

There was an instant of tearing pain. She cried out once, then lay beneath him numbly, feeling the shudders that shook him. With an agonized sound, he rolled off her.

"My God, Holly, I'm sorry—" His voice broke. With a choked sound he tried to gather her into his arms.

"No." She jerked over onto her side, her back to him, and huddled around herself like a child. He lay without touching her, fighting to control the emotions raging through him. When his hand smoothed back her hair, she flinched away. Gently, he rolled her rigid body over until she faced him.

"Holly—"

"If you're finished," she said in a clear, childlike voice, "I'd like to take a bath."

He would have preferred sarcasm or screams or self-pity to her simple statement of fact: he had made her feel unclean.

"Holly, don't." His voice was as ragged as hers had been clear. His hands trembled as he tried to comfort her.

With an inarticulate cry, she shoved him away and raced for the door. She was too upset to realize that it was still bolted shut. She tugged on the knob with both hands like a child, whimpering. Then she saw the bolt. She clawed at it, breaking her nails as she finally unlocked the door.

Linc's hand shot past her shoulder, slamming the door closed. His other hand flattened against the wall, holding her between his arms without actually touching her. His breath stirred her hair like a caress.

"No more," she whispered. "I should have told you I was Shannon and you should have believed I was a virgin. But I didn't and you didn't. We're even. Now let me go."

His voice was hoarse with anguish, his hands shaking as he stroked the midnight fall of her hair. "Holly—"

"My name is Shannon."

Linc made a noise not unlike hers as she had clawed at the bolt, but he didn't let her open the door. For long moments there was no sound but his broken breathing. When he finally spoke, his voice was so gentle it made tears burn behind her eyelids.

"I won't let you go, *niña*. You'd never come back. I can't live with that, with what I did to you, hurting you . . ."

Holly slumped against the door as though she wanted to sink into its wooden pores and vanish. He had hurt her, yes, but that was only part of the problem. The rest was a fundamental lack in her. "Forget it," she said dully. "It's not all your fault. I've been told I'm frigid. I finally believe it."

"Frigid?" He would have laughed if he could, but he was too shocked. "You are the most incredibly sensual woman I've ever known. That's one of the things that made it so hard for me to believe you were a virgin." He lifted her like a child in his arms, ignoring her protest and the stiffness of her body.

"Please, Linc," she whispered. "I can't take any more."

"I won't hurt you," he said, brushing the top of her head with his lips. "I promise I'll never hurt you like that again. I won't do anything you don't want me to. Trust me, Holly."

"I did . . ."

Her whisper was more for herself than for him, but he heard. He froze, finishing the rest of her sentence even though she said nothing at all: she had trusted him once, and he had violated that trust.

"I trusted someone called Holly," he said finally. "I want to trust her again. It's so easy to trust the first time, but the second . . . ?"

He waited for the longest moments of his life, straining to hear her answer. It did not come in words. Slowly she became less stiff in his arms. She did not rest her cheek on his chest, but neither did she show him only the back of her head. He carried her past the bed and into the bathroom.

The Jacuzzi steamed quietly, surrounded by lush ferns and wooden containers thick with exotic flowers. Lights hidden amid the greenery glowed like fallen stars. Slowly, he set her on her feet, supporting her until her legs stopped trembling. He took her hairbrush off the counter and brushed gently until there were no more tangles in her shining mass of hair. With deft motions, he gathered the strands into a single long braid.

She stood without moving, watching herself and him reflected in the mirrored walls. She did not see her own beauty, the feminine curve of breast and hip and waist, the tawny rose of nipples against her golden brown skin, the midnight plush of hair below her shadowed navel. She saw only Linc's face, gentle again, and the frightening strength that coiled beneath his skin with every motion of his body.

He secured the braid on top of her head with the same twist of gold she had worn before. When he was finished, he rested his hands lightly on her shoulders. His eyes met hers in the mirror. He looked at her as though he had never seen a woman before. She forgot to breathe, waiting for his hands to follow his eyes. When his hands stayed on her shoulders, she didn't know whether she was relieved or disappointed. Both, she admitted, and then was grateful that he had not touched her. She had learned to be afraid of his strength.

His fingers interlaced with hers as he led her toward the water. He flipped a switch. Jets of water made dazzling silver swirls in the Jacuzzi, while bubbles fizzed and sizzled like a conspiracy of laughter. He walked into the water, not turning toward her until he was clothed in brilliant, opaque bubbles. She felt another lessening of her tension, and realized that she had dreaded confronting his nakedness again. Somehow, he had known how she felt before she did.

"Watch the first step—" he began.

"—it's a lulu," she finished, surprising both of them with her wry words.

He smiled and lifted her fingertips to his lips. "It's also slippery." He let go of her hand before she could feel restrained in any way. "There are benches built in at two levels," he said. "You're probably tall enough to sit on the lower level without drowning in bubbles."

She hesitated, then sat at a midpoint on the lower level, not next to him and yet not as far away as she could get. Bubbles frothed up to her chin, hiding her behind their silver dance.

"Too cold?" he asked, seeing her lips tremble.

"Just nerves," she said in a strained voice.

"I won't—"

"I know," she said quickly. But did she?

Linc stretched out his long legs beneath the water, bracing himself on the lower bench on the opposite side. He let his head lie back on the padded rim and closed his eyes.

Holly watched him covertly, comparing his face with that of the ruthless stranger who had overwhelmed her. His mouth was no longer a thin, sardonic twist. His jaw was relaxed instead of tightened in a grim thrust of male aggression. His unfair strength was concealed beneath a gleaming froth that fizzed and shifted each second. She shivered again, a tremor of muscles that were slowly relaxing. With a sigh, she rested her head against the rim and let the water's heat claim her.

For several minutes there was no sound but that of the bright water seething over their bodies.

The swirling water was alive with mischief, teasing her legs with a promise of support, then gently floating her toward the center of the Jacuzzi. She braced her arms along the rim, feeling gooseflesh form as the cooler air of the room poured over her skin. Her legs floated out and bumped against Linc. She froze. His eyes didn't open, nor did his position change. The third time her feet drifted into his legs, she made a frustrated sound. The Jacuzzi had been built for Linc's six-foot four-inch length. He could brace himself comfortably, but she could not.

"Go ahead and put your feet on my leg," he suggested without opening his eyes.

She hesitated, then let her legs float out. His hair tickled slightly as the soles of her feet fitted themselves to the muscular curve of his thigh. She waited, half-expecting the water to carry her off again, but it did not. His firm flesh braced her securely. The heat and soothing murmur of the water slowly unraveled her tension. With a sigh, she rested her head against the padded rim and let her mind empty until it drifted as aimlessly as a bubble.

After a long time, she opened her eyes. He was watching her with a gentleness and regret that made her throat ache. His arm came out of the water, reaching toward her. She didn't move away. He didn't touch her. Instead, he leaned forward and took a towel from a stack between two flowering plants. He stood, wrapping the towel around his hips as he came out of the water. When he was on the last step, he looked back down at her.

"Better?" he asked quietly.

She nodded.

He went to a cupboard and took out one of his huge bath towels. "Time to get out. Too much of this will turn your brain into pudding."

"And your skin into a relief map," said Holly, holding out her wrinkled hands.

She hesitated before she stepped into the towel he was holding out for her. He rubbed her dry with impersonal hands and then wrapped the towel around her, covering her from collarbone to ankles. She shivered as her body adjusted to being out of the water. Or was it being so close to him that she could count the drops of water on his body that made her tremble? She was startled by her impulse to lick up each silver gleam with the tip of her tongue. The thought was as mesmerizing as the hot water had been.

"Where did you hide that oil?" he asked.

For a moment she didn't realize that he had spoken to her. "What?" She forced herself to look away from the bright rivulets of water that escaped down his flat stomach, only to be caught again in the crisp line of hair that began beneath his navel.

"Oil," he repeated patiently.

"Oil. Ummm." Holly glanced around the room, but her eyes were too filled with Linc to see anything else.

"I think I left you in there too long," he said.

She smiled faintly, echoing the laughter in his voice. Then she spotted an amber container. "There."

He picked up the bottle and walked over to the bed. When he turned, she was still standing in the bathroom. He waited, saying nothing. Slowly she walked toward him.

"If you'd rather stay on your feet," he said, "that's fine. But you'll get your rubdown either way, or you'll have skin like a horned toad by morning."

"What about you?" she asked in a small voice, not meeting his eyes.

For an instant he looked surprised. He handed the bottle to her and lay facedown on the bed. "Ready when you are," he said matter-of-factly.

She poured oil into her hands, warmed it and bent over him without getting on the bed. She rubbed oil into his back and shoulders, trying to ignore the shift and gleam of his muscles and the tingling that began in her palms. When she reached the towel, she stopped, shifted to the foot of the bed and began rubbing oil into his feet and calves. She worked briskly, avoiding the possibility of sensual pleasure. The further up his legs she progressed, the more difficult it became for her. She stopped just above his knees.

He rolled onto his side. "Thanks. I can get the rest."

She watched, fascinated by the gleam of oil spreading over him.

"Your turn."

His tone was casual, almost indifferent. He poured oil in his hands to warm and waited. She lay on her stomach. Other than her shoulders, arms and feet, the thick towel covered all of her. He smoothed oil into her skin, gently kneading down each arm to her fingertips, then back up again. He repeated the process several times, until she relaxed beneath his hands. Only then did he sit next to her on the bed. As she shifted to adjust to his presence, his hands moved between her shoulder blades, loosening the towel.

Tension crept into the line of her back. He spread oil over her skin with slow, impersonal movements of his hands that reassured and soothed her. With a tiny sigh, she relaxed again. He kneaded down her back, his strong hands demanding nothing of her, yet giving her a sensual pleasure that was slowly turning her bones to water.

She made a tiny sound of disappointment when he stopped. He smiled and moved down to the end of the bed. He took her foot between his hands, rubbing firmly so that he would not tickle her. His hands worked up her calf, massaging the muscles that were firm rather than hard, a woman's strength, more gentle than a man's yet just as enduring.

When he finished with the calf, he went beneath the towel to the flesh above her knee. The towel loosened with each stroke of his hands. He kneaded with fingers and palms, surrounding her thigh with warm pressure. Then he worked down to her toes and back up.

Gradually she stopped tensing every time his hands went above her knees. He had shown no inclination to force any intimacy on her. She sighed and shifted her position, loosening the towel still more. She drifted as she had in the water, her mind empty, her body caressed by warm sensations.

"Time to roll over," he said easily.

She murmured tiny complaints at being disturbed. As she rolled over, the towel came undone. She gathered it up hastily, only to have him take it from her fingers.

"I'll get you a dry one," he said, not even looking at the gleaming length of her body.

He returned in a minute with another, much smaller towel which he draped over her. Then he began at her fingertips again, smoothing away tension and self-consciousness with each stroke. He carefully avoided going any lower than her collarbone. Soon she forgot that she wore only a small towel and a fragrant shimmer of oil. She relaxed and gave herself over to the pleasure of his touch once more.

He went to the end of the bed and again began rubbing oil into her feet and legs. He slid his hands beneath the towel, kneading the smooth curve of her thighs, savoring the silk of her skin. He eased his weight onto the bed, straddling her without confining her, never breaking the easy rhythms of the massage as his hands slid up and over her hips, over the flat muscles of her stomach, up to a point just short of her breasts and then down again, leaving behind a dizzying spiral of sensation that showed as a flush just beneath her skin.

The sure, slow pressure of his hands on her body made her want to stop time, to float suspended forever while his hands soothed and set her on fire at the same time. The gentle torment was endless, his hands advancing and retreating just short of intimacy, the towel sliding over her breasts with each breath, hot wires of sensation radiating from the pit of her stomach. She moaned without knowing it as his hands slid up the inside of her thighs, then curved aside from the heat between her legs, a heat she wanted him to touch.

"Linc . . ."

His hands stopped instantly. She felt the outline of his fingers pressed against her stomach. His weight shifted as he moved to get off the bed. She sat up quickly, not caring that the towel slid off, leaving her naked. She took his hands and put them back on her stomach. As he closed his eyes, she felt the shudder that went through him. Suddenly she realized that his casual words and gestures had been an act to reassure her; he wanted her as much as he ever had, perhaps more.

"You don't have to," he said.

She hesitated and knew that he felt the tightness of her body against his palms. "I can't guarantee anything," she whispered. "I don't know what to do . . ."

He bent forward and kissed her eyelids. "You don't have to do anything at all, *niña*," he murmured, tracing her eyelashes with the tip of his tongue. "Let me pleasure you."

A tiny pool of oil warmed in his palm, sending up a fragrance that was clean and tantalizing. He began at her fingertips again, but this time he went from her shoulders to her waist. She gasped when his hands flowed over her breasts and moved on as though he had not noticed the taut rise of her nipples. His hands kneaded down her stomach toward her thighs. She held her breath, waiting for him to find and caress the aching warmth between her legs.

Again he disappointed her, fingers sliding by as he went down her thighs, setting fire to her skin. When his hands drifted upward again, fingertips teasing, she unconsciously moved her legs apart, silently asking for his touch. Her breath caught in her throat, only to be let out in a groan when he did no more than let his palm glide over her, ruffling the midnight gleam of hair.

She opened her eyes, saw him alive with the pleasure of watching her. When he sensed her look, he smiled and let his hands move slowly from her navel to the tips of her breasts. The nipples changed beneath his fingertips, telling him vividly of her arousal. His breath came out in a rush as he buried his face between her breasts.

After a long moment he lifted his head and kissed her lips with an unhurried pleasure that made her tremble. He lowered his head to trace her nipples with lazy strokes of his tongue. His teeth closed delicately around her taut flesh, drawing gasps of pleasure from her. He caressed the length of her body, pausing to taste each new curve of flesh, his hands moving in slow, undemanding rhythms.

When his teeth found the softness of her inner thigh, she twisted slowly against him and threaded her fingers into his thick hair. She felt an agony of suspense as his mouth hesitated, then moved upward brushing aside her midnight hair, savoring all the textures of her desire until she was shaken by waves of pleasure.

Only then did he resume his languid exploration of her body. His tongue teased her sensitive navel, made her breasts ache with pleasure, gently tormented her lips as his hand curled down her body until he could tangle his fingers in her silky hair, seeking the incredible softness inside her. She made a sound deep in her throat and moved hungrily against him, asking. He froze, gripped in a vise of relief and passion that almost overwhelmed him. It was the first time she had reached out to him since he had taken in anger what she had wanted to give in love.

"What's wrong?" she whispered, her hands sliding over his face, seeking the answer.

"I was afraid you'd never want me again," he said raggedly. "But you do . . . your body can't lie, *niña.*"

His fingers stroked intimately, rhythms that stole the breath out of her throat in a broken sigh. Her hips moved against his hand with a sinuous demand that shredded his control. He closed his eyes, fighting to master his fierce response to her sensuality. When he opened his eyes, she was watching him.

"I'm not afraid of your strength anymore."

Despite her words, he gathered her against his body as though she were more fragile than her new trust of him. Her hands slid down his back, pulling him closer, savoring the power of him, a power that he held in check for her. She took his hand and guided it down her body. The intimacy of his fingers was no longer a shock, but a revelation of her own sensuality.

The languid weakness that had pervaded her condensed into a tension that had nothing to do with fear. A fine mist bloomed over her skin and her breath shortened. She moved against him with liquid warmth, melting over him with small moans. When her fingers found the towel that was still wrapped around him, she tugged it off impatiently, wanting to feel nothing but his skin sliding over hers. This time when she touched him, she did not retreat.

As her fingers closed around him, he couldn't control the groan that shuddered through him. He rubbed against her warmth, sending a sunburst of fire through her. She twisted against him, trying to touch all of him at once, seeking something that would end the beautiful agony she was suspended in. She spoke his name repeatedly in a litany of desire, asking him to be part of her.

"Are you sure?" he whispered, controlling his own consuming need to be inside her. "I couldn't stand hurting you again."

She opened herself with a trust that almost shattered him. He guided her legs around his waist, teased her with his body until she cried out and melted all over him again. At that instant he took her with the same gentle care he had used to seduce her, advancing by increments, always giving less of himself than she wanted until she called his name in a fierce demand for more.

Finally he became wholly a part of her, moving slowly, deeply, watching her surprise and wonder as her own sensuality consumed her. Then he bent down and drank the cries of ecstasy from her lips, letting himself drown in her sweet rain.

10

Holly woke up in the morning snuggled along Linc's powerful body. Their legs were tangled together, his arms were around her and the hair on his chest both tickled and delighted her. She burrowed against him with unself-conscious pleasure, enjoying the intimacy of his hard thigh between her legs, his muscular chest warming her breasts, the strong tendons of his neck beneath her palm. She moved closer to him, savoring the changing pressure of his body on hers.

Memories of their lovemaking sparked through her, a time of sleeping and waking in warm darkness to the feel of his mouth loving her, passion breaking over them like a desert storm, shaking them until they cried out and held each other in a pleasure as fierce as lightning. Sleeping again and waking with a smile because even in the dark she knew he was near, she could taste him, touch him, pull his male strength around her until he filled her and lightning rained down again.

Heat uncurled in the pit of her stomach. She tried to lie quietly, but the temptations of his body were too great. She stretched against him sensually, smiling and murmuring softly, her body so sensitized to his presence that it was almost painful. When his arms tightened around her, pulling her onto his chest, she shivered with pleasure and anticipation.

"Good morning," she said, smiling.

He looked at her for a long time, his hazel eyes dark with emotion. "You're even more beautiful in the morning," he said in a husky voice. Then, "My God, what am I going to do . . . ?"

The tension in his voice came from more than his response to her body. She knew he was thinking of his mother and stepmother, as cruel as they were beautiful. One night could not erase the past, however much she and Linc wanted it to.

"Trust me," she breathed, then bent her head and traced his lips with the tip of her tongue. "I love you, Linc."

He groaned and buried his fingers in her thick hair, holding her mouth against his in a passionate kiss that ended only when the ringing phone on the bedside table became too irritating to ignore. He tore his lips away with a pungent curse that she silently seconded. His finger raked over the switch, activating the speaker.

"People usually give up after ten rings," he snarled.

There was a pause, then Roger's laughter floated up out of the phone. "Good morning to you, too. Is Shannon around, or did you have her for a midnight snack?"

Linc raised an eyebrow in Holly's direction.

She sighed. "Good morning, Roger," she said, trying to ignore Linc's expression, changing as she watched, stopping just short of the hard-faced stranger.

"Sorry if I caught you at an inappropriate moment. We leave for Cabo San Lucas in an hour."

"That's not enough warning—" she began.

"It's all I have. Hurricane Giselle is closing in on the cape. If we're lucky, we'll get five days. If not, only two.

Giselle and the fashion seasons wait for no man. I've packed up your stuff here. Meet us at the airport in an hour."

Holly made a sound of frustration. "Can't I fly down after you have everything in place?"

"It's already in place. I sent the technicians there when Hidden Springs was rained out." He hesitated. "Really, love, I *am* sorry. But we're behind schedule as it is. If we don't get the shots we need, the Romance campaign is in the loo."

"Get another model," said Linc in a clear, hard voice.

Roger's laugh was clipped. "You're joking. Shannon *is* the Romance campaign."

Linc looked at Holly, waiting.

"I'll be at the airport in an hour," she said tonelessly, and flipped the switch before Roger could reply.

Linc got out of bed in a single, savage motion. He stood with his back to her, every muscle tense. When he spoke, his voice showed the effort it took to control himself. "Why?"

"It's my job," she said simply.

"Quit."

"I'm under contract."

"Break it."

"No."

Slowly he turned around. His eyes searched hers. "Is it so important for you to be wanted by more than one man?"

"That has nothing to do with it!"

"It did for the two 'models' I knew," he said coldly.

"They weren't typical," said Holly in an angry voice. "Women who call themselves models and sell sex on the side don't last long. What they're peddling is nothing special. It can be found in any town big enough to have a street corner."

His disbelief showed in the sardonic curl of his mouth. He watched her with eyes that were nearly dark, as opaque as stones at the bottom of a river.

She stood up and walked over to him. "Real models work on their feet and they work hard. They hold poses in impossible positions for hours on end and smile convincingly on command. They don't eat when they're hungry, they exercise when they'd rather be asleep, they work long hours under miserable conditions and then put up with insults from ignorant, prejudiced people who think model is another name for whore." She took a deep, shaking breath. "That simply isn't true. Fashion is a business. Models are part of it."

"Some business. Showing off overpriced clothes for rich women."

"Wrong again," she snapped. "High fashion is a very small part of the industry. And it is an industry, Linc. Everybody who wears clothes is part of it. Even you. Fashion figures in the Gross National Product just like cars, candy bars and computers."

He ran his fingers through his hair in a frustrated gesture. "Fine," he said grudgingly. "Fashion is a flaming national asset. Is it more important to you than being with me?"

"Why don't you come to Cabo San Lucas with me?" she countered. "Then we'll not only be together, but you'll also see what modeling is—and *isn't*."

"I have work to do. Real work."

"And just how is raising overpriced horses for rich men more important work than mine?" she challenged.

"Raising horses isn't work, it's my life." His expression changed, more surprise than anger. "Is that what you're trying to say—modeling is your *life?*"

"It's part of me."

"More important than what we could have?"

"I'm not making you choose between me and your work," she said desperately. "Why are you making me choose?"

He turned away and began pulling clothes out of his closet. "I'll drive you to the airport."

She crossed the room quickly and stood behind him.

Tentatively, her fingers traced the muscled ridges of his back, then her arms slid around his body in a hug. "I love you," she said softly.

She felt him stiffen, then let out his breath in a long sigh. Gently, he unwrapped her arms and turned to face her.

"Don't love me," he said, his voice rich with anger and sadness. "That will hurt you more than anything I could do to you. And in spite of what I think of models, I don't want you hurt."

"I don't understand," she whispered.

He gathered her hands and kissed her fingertips very gently, watching her with eyes that were too dark. "Love is a game for masochists, niña. You can't win, you can't stay even and you can't get out of the game."

"I don't believe that," she said shakily.

"You will." He released her hands. "Get dressed. You don't want to be late for work."

Holly smiled brilliantly, belying the hot needles of fatigue that stitched across her shoulders and made her thighs quiver beneath the flowing, sea-green gown. Behind her reared the desolate splendor of the rocks that were Cabo San Lucas, shimmering beneath a brutal tropical heat. A desultory breeze lifted clinging folds of chiffon, making the fragile cloth ripple and gleam, echoing the waves swelling toward the heated sand. The net of diamonds around her throat sparkled like drops of water flung from a breaking wave. Late-afternoon light turned her eyes to gold and made even the jagged rocks look velvety.

"Right," said the director's clipped voice. "Again. But get Shannon's hair first."

Holly put her hands on the small of her back and rubbed, trying to stretch muscles that were cramped from hours of bending and turning and posing on the uneven ground. The motion sequence she was doing now was easier physically, but mentally it was infinitely worse. Walking down to the water and standing ankle-deep in foam was easy. Stepping into Roger's arms and looking eager for his embrace was not. It was bad enough to be held by a man who was not Linc; to be kissed was unbearable. She wished Roger had chosen a stranger, rather than himself, to be the Royce male model. It would have been easier to ignore desire in a stranger's eyes.

She stood patiently while the stylist fussed over her long hair. Whatever he did, the wind would shortly undo. But Roger wanted her hair unbound, rippling and lifting in the wind like a midnight cloud. Very effective and romantic, if it ever worked. Air moving off the sea was damp, salty and erratic, turning her hair into tangled strings and requiring her to hold poses until her muscles cramped as the photographer waited for just the right amount of wind. At least the still photos were finished. For that small blessing she was grateful.

After a final sweep with the brush, the stylist trotted off the set.

"Remember, Shannon," called the director, "this is supposed to simply *ooze* sensuality. 'When you meet the man of your dreams, be wearing a Royce.' That's the theme. It's the man of your dreams walking out of the water, not some blooming stranger."

"I've read the script," called Holly impatiently, letting her temper show. She had done more of this in the last five days than she had in the previous five years.

"Then bloody well act like it!" shot back the director, his voice an echo of Roger's British tones. "Action!"

Holly followed the directions in the script automatically, turning and dipping and arching her back, looking sad and wistful and alone, a woman longing for her lover. The expression came easily; she had been aching for Linc since he had left her at the airport five days before. She had called him twice. The housekeeper had answered both times. Linc had not returned the calls.

"Makeup!" called the director.

With a sigh, Holly dropped her arms and waited for the makeup man to come out and repair whatever damage the director had spotted. Roger, who was a hundred feet out in the water, waist-deep in the incandescent trail of the sun, came in and stood by her side.

"Under the eyes," instructed the director through the bullhorn. "Gloss the lips while you're about it."

Roger stood very close, examining her critically. "You really should try sleeping at night, Shannon."

"I do try," she said calmly.

"Then try succeeding."

Holly started to speak, but had to hold still for the gloss to be applied. The hairstylist hurried up, ever alert for the opportunity to brush Holly's hair into a flyaway cloud of black silk. The makeup man went to work erasing unwanted shadows.

"I do succeed," she said the instant her lips were free.

"Rot. I've heard you pacing your balcony all night, every night."

She said nothing. There was nothing she could say. She had slept only a few hours a night since Linc had dropped her at the airport without so much as a good-bye kiss. "I'll tiptoe. Sorry to keep you awake."

"I'm more worried about your sleep than mine. I don't want the Royce Reflection to look like a half-starved, overworked waif." He made an impatient gesture when she started to argue. "I'm the one who has had to take in your dresses down here. Twice."

"Sorry," she said again.

Roger swore. "I don't want apologies, I want you happy! It's that damned cowboy, isn't it?"

Her face changed despite her efforts to show nothing.

"Bloody hell. I knew he was too rough for you."

"It's the humidity here that's too rough," she said lightly, pulling her professional smile on like a mask. "A regular sauna. Guess I'll never make a tropic princess."

"It can be just as humid in Palm Springs," Roger pointed out.

Holly just smiled. The makeup man finished and left as silently as he had come. She hardly noticed. She had seen a tall figure walking down to the beach beyond the roped-off area, a man who moved like Linc. Her heart stopped, then beat frantically. She stared out over the ocean, but could see only a well-built, graceful man silhouetted against the incandescent wake of the sun. He dove into the brilliant colors and vanished.

"What's wrong, love? You're shaking." Roger turned away and called to the director. "Wrap it up. She's had enough for today."

"No," said Holly quickly, furious that just the shadow of a powerful man could upset her so thoroughly. This had to end. She could not go on like a sleepwalker blundering through a dissolving dream. She owed Roger more than the shell of Shannon. In the past she had pretended that Linc was nearby when she performed for the camera. She would pretend again, using new memories as she had used old ones. "This is the best time. The light is like honey."

"There'll be another afternoon tomorrow," said Roger.

"The hurricane won't stall forever. Tomorrow might be too late." She turned and called out to the director. "Ready!"

And she was. She pulled her memories of Linc around her like a veil, wrapping herself in shimmering sensuality. She remembered the moment when she woke up in his arms, his warm tongue teasing her lips, making her smile.

Jerry, who was on the sidelines taking still photos for the magazine campaign, crowed triumphantly, "That's it! God, babe, that's fantastic!"

The director shouted at Jerry to be quiet, then shrugged. As long as it didn't bother the model, noise didn't matter. The sound would be dubbed in later.

Holly heard Jerry and the director as though they were at the end of a long tunnel. Wrapped in memories, she radiated sensual hunger that was all the more compelling because her face was shadowed with loneliness. Wind swirled around her, caressing her skin, lifting her hair, billowing the endless layers of sea-foam chiffon, revealing the perfect curves of her legs. Light poured over her like molten gold.

Roger, wet with salt water, his hair in artistic disarray, walked out of the breakers toward her. A black mask and snorkel dangled from his left hand. Slanting light picked up the gleam of water trickling down his tanned skin. Black swim briefs clung to his athletic body.

Holly watched him walk forward and mentally fitted Linc's likeness over Roger. It didn't work. She closed her eyes and tried again. The director's frustrated comments bounced off her concentration. She held out her hand and let herself be pulled into Roger's arms. His head bent slowly toward her. He kissed her with cool lips. Then his arms tightened and his tongue went between her teeth. After an instant of shock, she angrily pushed him away.

"Cut!" yelled the director, as he strode down the beach. "Shannon, what the devil is wrong with you?"

"Ask Roger," she said tightly.

Roger sighed. "Sorry, love. You're such an overwhelming temptation." He smiled charmingly, but there was real hunger beneath his polished surface. "Women who look like you need more than kissing," he said quietly.

He took the director's arm and walked the angry man back up the beach, talking to him in soothing tones. Holly didn't bother to listen. She closed her eyes and fought her instinctive revulsion at being kissed so intimately by any man but Linc. She reminded herself that actresses kissed men all the time—and hated most of them, if the gossip were true. Surely she could be kissed by a good friend without freezing up.

She heard the technicians rushing around up the beach, compensating for the fading light. She sensed their quiet, frantic speed. The lighting of the scene was crucial: her face had to be illuminated mostly by the setting sun; Roger's face had to be almost entirely in shadow; and the sunset behind them had to radiate all the colors of sensuality. To achieve the three effects at once was a feat that had the light men cursing and tearing out their hair.

"Is Roger in place?" yelled the director.

Holly shaded her eyes and looked into the dazzling reflections left by the setting sun. The blaze of light blinded her, but she could make out a masculine form walking out of the waves toward her.

"Ready," she shouted, fighting the coldness creeping up from her stomach. She didn't want Roger to touch her again.

"Action!"

Once again she pulled her memories around her and went through the motions of a woman watching the man of her dreams emerge from the sea. Once again she held out her hand to him almost shyly, blinded by the dying sun. But before his fingers touched hers, memories and reality collided.

"*Linc . . . !*"

He took her hand and pressed her palm against his lips. Wind caught her dress and her hair, wrapping him in a sensual caress as he pulled her into his arms. His lips were firm, sweet and salt, better than her memories. She flowed against him, clinging to him without reservation, abandoning herself to his potent warmth. When she felt his tongue caress hers, she thought she would die of the pleasure coursing through her.

"Cut! That was perfect, but I believe in insurance. One more time. Hey, out there! Cut!"

Slowly, Linc lifted his head. His eyes were hooded, his mouth still hungry.

"They think you're Roger," she said breathlessly.

"I know. I've been watching Roger kiss you all afternoon." His voice was as hard as his eyes. Before she could answer, his arms closed around her like iron bars. His mouth came down swiftly, anticipating resistance.

She responded with a force that equaled his, dragging his head down to her lips, probing his mouth with a hungry tongue. She didn't care about the people on the beach, the expensive dress whipping in the wind, the warm sea creaming around her calves. She only knew that she was starving for the taste and feel of the man who had walked out of the sun to hold her in his arms.

"Shannon! Who the hell is that out there with you?" called Roger indignantly. "How did he get past the ropes!"

Holly ignored the shout, ignored everything but her ravenous need to drink Linc's presence into every pore. When he tried to end the kiss, she clung more tightly. With bruising strength, he jerked free of her arms and walked back into the incandescent sea.

"Shannon, are you all right?" shouted Roger, running down the beach to her. "Shannon? Can you hear me?"

"I'm fine," she said shakily. "That was Linc."

Roger's lips turned into a thin, downward-curving line. "I should have guessed. You kissed him like he was Neptune come to claim you." He took her face between his hands, saw the sensual excitement blazing in her eyes and the hunger trembling in her bruised lips. "If you had kissed me like that," he said tightly, "I wouldn't have walked away. Shannon, let me make—"

"Stop it, Roger. Stop it!" She jerked away, shivering, and stared into the sea where Linc had vanished. She saw nothing but the distorted, blinding reflections of the dying sun.

The director stormed up. "This is a zoo, a damned zoo! I get the best shot of my life and Jerry keeps yapping that it's the wrong man!"

"Couldn't you tell?" said Roger irritably.

"Look," said the director, his voice clipped. "A tall,

well-built chap walks out of the surf and kisses Shannon, right? It's been happening all day, right? The only difference is that this last time the light was perfect, the wind was perfect and the two of them damn near melted the lenses off the bloody cameras."

"You couldn't see the face, the difference in height?" said Roger.

"You're in silhouette, your face is in shadow. You have to bend over to kiss her. So did he. Am I supposed to notice that one of you bent down a few centimeters farther than the other?" The director added a few words that crackled with frustration, then sighed. "Right. One more time."

He strode back up the beach, yelling through his bullhorn. Technicians scattered. One of the light men walked up to him, pointed to the sun—now barely a fingernail above the horizon—and then toward the beach where lighting equipment waited amid a tangle of cables. The director made an angry gesture and waved everybody into place.

Holly turned toward the sea, but saw only Roger's retreating figure. She looked up the beach, beyond the ropes where people stared and pointed at her and the cameras. There was no tall, powerful man among them. There was no one at all between her and the shimmering expanse of sand and rock leading to the cliff-top hotel. It was as though she had conjured up Linc out of her own tearing loneliness, but he had been too potent to be held by her spell. He had pulled all the colors of her desire around him . . . and vanished.

"Wake up, Shannon!" shouted the director. "I said *action!*"

Empty, she turned to wait for the wrong man to walk out of the sea to her.

Like a nightmare, the scene repeated itself endlessly, the dark outline of a man coming out of the scarlet sea, the touch, the kiss. The only variation was the draining light and the increasing coldness of her body. When the director finally decided that there was no point in continuing, the sky held only a faint blush of orange.

Shivering, Holly walked beyond the reach of the luminous waves. Roger walked beside her, watching her, measuring her strain in the harsh lines of her face. She should have looked less appealing, haggard, but did not. She simply looked aloof, mysterious, her beauty heightened by the darkness that moved beneath her surface.

When the director would have come over to her, Roger waved him off. He led her through the bustle of technicians to the tent she used for dressing. Inside the tent hung three more dresses just like the one she wore, insurance against the random leap of waves. He began unfastening her dress with the deft, impersonal fingers of a man who made his living clothing women.

Abruptly, Holly came out of her daze. "No," she said, moving away from him.

"Don't be ridiculous. I've undressed you a thousand times—and dressed you, for that matter."

"Not this time."

"I'll wait outside, then."

"You don't have to wait."

"I'm taking you to dinner. That's an order, not an invitation. I'll be damned if I'm going to take in those dresses again."

"But Linc—"

"If Linc wanted to be here, he would be here," said Roger coldly.

Holly looked away, unable to meet the anger and compassion in Roger's blue eyes. "He's probably at the hotel, waiting for me to finish," she said.

Roger grabbed a cordless phone off a wardrobe trunk and turned his back. "Change your clothes."

She hesitated, then began taking off the clinging dress. She heard Roger talk to the hotel desk and waited with held breath while Linc's room was rung. No one answered. He asked for Lincoln McKenzie to be paged in the hotel restaurants and lobby. No one responded.

"Right," said Roger, putting the phone back on the trunk. "He must be having dinner somewhere else."

Numbly, Holly pulled over her head the soft, loose cotton float that she had worn down to the beach that morning. Roger walked her to her room, making conversation that she didn't really hear.

"I'll pick you up in forty-five minutes," Roger said, putting his hand on her arm to prevent her from slipping through the partially open door.

"Roger, I'm not hungry."

"How would you know? You haven't tried eating for five days. You might find you're starving." He looked closely at her. His eyes changed, darker now, the color of twilight. "If not food, then something else. Invite me in, Shannon. You'll never be hungry again, I guarantee it. You know how good I am with a woman's smooth body."

"Don't, Roger," she whispered. "Please don't. I—" The rest of her words were lost in a gasp as the door was jerked open from inside.

"I'm afraid you'll have to put it on hold," said Linc in a lazy voice, but his eyes were cold as he looked at her. He shifted his glance to Roger. "Don't worry, I can't stay long. You'll understand if I don't invite you in," he finished, giving Roger a sardonic smile. "But I do appreciate your warming her up. Like I said, I don't have much time."

He pulled Holly inside and slammed the door.

"That wasn't necessary," said Holly tightly. "I've said no to Roger before without your help."

"Really?" he said, reaching for her. "I didn't hear a damn thing that sounded like no."

"Linc—" She turned her face aside, avoiding his lips.

"What's the matter? Wrong man?" His expression was harsh. He let go of her and reached for the door. "I'll call Roger."

"That's not it!"

"Oh?" His voice was still lazy, his eyes like polished stone. "Then what is it? Do you need a camera to perform?" He shrugged. "That shouldn't be hard to arrange. This is Mexico, after all."

"Why are you doing this?" she whispered.

"Doing what? I cut short my trip to Texas—"

"I didn't know—"

"You didn't ask about *my* work," he said curtly. "I was looking over some Arabians in Texas, but I couldn't stop thinking about you, about what you'd said. I realized I didn't know what professional models did." His lips twisted in a travesty of a smile. "So I chartered a plane to Cabo San Lucas and spent the afternoon watching your half-naked boss kiss you and listening to the men around the rope speculate about what you're like in bed. Hell of a way to sell clothes."

"I'm glad it was so exciting for the spectators," she said icily. "For me, it was about as romantic as cleaning fish."

Linc looked startled.

"They were stage kisses," she continued in her hard Shannon voice. "All show and no go. Except once, when you walked out of the sea and kissed me and I felt like I had fallen into the sun."

His expression changed as her words sliced through his anger. "I doubt that Roger would agree about stage kisses and cleaning fish."

"That is Roger's problem," she said, clipping each word.

Linc's hand rubbed through his hair. "And my problem?" he suggested quietly. "Is Roger my problem, too?"

"Only if you want him to be. I won't play games, Linc. I love you too much for that."

"Then why won't you quit modeling?" His voice was neither angry nor hard, simply curious.

"Wrong question. What you really want to know is

why I won't destroy half of myself to please you. That's not love, Linc. That's hate."

"But—"

"If I asked you to kill the part of you that loves the ranch, what would you call it?"

There was a long silence. Then, "Love you, love your modeling. Is that it?"

"Modeling is a part of me just as the ranch is a part of you. If you can't accept that, then you can't accept *me*."

"I didn't come here to argue."

"Then what did you come here for?"

"You know what. You knew it when you kissed me."

"Is that all you want from me?" Her eyes were wide. Shadows moved in their tawny depths.

"It's the same thing you want from me," he said, slowly gathering her close to him. He groaned deep in his throat as his hands felt her warmth through the thin cotton dress. "Kiss me again, Holly. Send us both falling into the sun."

"But—"

"Tomorrow," he said thickly, pulling her against his thighs, letting her feel his need. "We'll talk tomorrow."

11

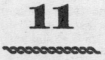

Holly awoke before her alarm went off. It was always like that when she was working; she hated the alarm so much that she got up early just to avoid it. She eased out from under Linc's arm and pushed in the alarm button on the clock. Linc muttered and moved restlessly, seeking her in his sleep. She slipped beneath his arm again. Still asleep, he gathered her against himself and sighed deeply.

Except for the golden glow of a night-light across the room, it was dark. Holly savored the stolen moments of his warmth, his arm wrapped around her hips, her lips tickled by the hair on his chest. She knew she should get out of bed, do her exercises, shower, wash and set her hair; but she had missed him too much to leave him easily now.

"I love you," she whispered, a bare thread of sound in the silence.

She didn't expect an answer. Even if he had been awake, he would not have said what she wanted to hear. Uneasiness twisted through her, cold frissons of fear that she couldn't ignore. He had made love to her during the night, touching her deeply, teaching her to respond to the call of his body. Each time had been better for her, a sensual progression that finally consumed them both. He had given her the most intense pleasure imaginable, and then doubled it, showing her the limitations of her own imagination with each sweet movement of his body over hers. There had been no end to her wanting, or his.

She wanted him now with an intensity that frightened her. He was as necessary to her as her eyes or her hands, yet he could leave so suddenly. She felt vulnerable, afraid, as though she was alone in a desert storm, lightning raining down closer each time, and the only shelter around locked and bolted against her. If Linc loved her, it wouldn't matter that he was sinking into her, becoming a part of her, for he would cherish her and protect her from her own vulnerability to him. He would open the door to himself and not lock it again until she was safe inside. If he loved her.

But he didn't.

It wasn't just the words he didn't say that warned her. For all his passionate intensity, for all his consummate skill in touching her, the laughter and gentle caring they had shared at Hidden Springs was gone. She gave herself to him, mind and body, and in return he gave her . . . pleasure . . . body without mind. He hid from her behind physical fires that grew greater each time they made love. She was being consumed, not renewed.

Yet she wanted him, for he had sunk into her very bones. She loved him, for he was a part of her.

The clock ticked, marking off dark minutes. Holly lifted Linc's arm and gradually eased away from him. She pulled on the first piece of clothing she found— Linc's shirt—and began her morning exercises. She worked quietly, stretching and toning muscles both for her own satisfaction and for the camera's relentlessly critical eye. She was nearly finished when Linc rolled over and woke up.

"Good Lord, Holly, it's not even dawn," he groaned, sitting up and turning on the small bedside light. He stared at her damp, flushed face in disbelief.

"Welcome to—the glamorous world—of models," she said between sit-ups. "Twenty-four. Twenty-five." She lay back with a small groan, then rolled over and began doing push-ups.

"All that for a beautiful body?" he said skeptically.

"For a—*healthy*—body."

For several minutes there was nothing but the sound of her counting. Finally she sighed and switched to a cross-legged position. Slowly she bent over until her forehead touched the floor. She repeated the exercise several times, holding the stretched position a few seconds longer each time.

"Which is worst," he asked, "the sit-ups, push-ups or forehead-on-the-floor?"

"Yes."

He looked puzzled, then he laughed. She stared at him, realizing it was the first genuine laughter she had heard from him since he had found out she was Holly Shannon North.

"I can think of more pleasant ways to exercise," he said lazily, watching his shirt ride high up on her thighs.

"So can I," she retorted. "That's why I'm going to take a shower next."

He climbed out of the bed, his naked skin gleaming in the dim light, his desire obvious. He sat cross-legged on the floor facing her, so close that their legs rubbed and her hair fell across his thighs when she bent over. She looked up. His expression made her catch her breath. Long fingers began undoing the buttons on the shirt she had borrowed.

"I have to shower, do my hair and get to the set," she said, her voice breathless from more than her exercise.

"When?" he asked, unbuttoning as he spoke.

"I should be in the shower right now."

The shirt fell away, revealing the golden curves of her breasts, nipples already tight with desire. His fingertips touched her as delicately as a kiss, then his palms moved over her waist and hips, hungry for the soft textures of her body. His hunger for her made fluid warmth curl throughout her body. When his hand slid up her thighs to taste her softness, she felt herself come undone.

"So you do want me," he said, his voice suddenly as ragged as his breathing. "Come sit in my lap," he said, lifting her legs over his. "Shhh. It won't take long. You can shower afterward."

"We were supposed to talk," she said, trying and failing to control her own breathing.

"We will," he said, guiding her hips. "Tomorrow."

Her objections were lost in the pleasure that shook her when he became part of her again. With a low moan, she began moving over him.

"All right, that's a wrap!" called the director. He looked at Roger, elegant in a sage-colored safari shirt. "Unless you want to try a few takes for Desert Designs . . . ?"

"The Desert Designs campaign isn't due for six weeks. Let's not be greedy. Besides, with the edge of that hurricane finally moving in, the sky doesn't make a very convincing desert backdrop." Roger turned to his assistant. "Break out the peppermints."

Holly heard the words with a feeling of acute relief. If Roger was passing out mints, the shoot was over. It was a Royce tradition. She accepted the first mint, smiled at the crew and left the set.

They had been working for nine straight days. Every muscle in her body ached. At least Roger hadn't been complaining about the fit of her clothes, though. Her appetite had returned with Linc, and had stayed, as he had stayed. She looked beyond the roped-off area, seeking him. Almost all the spectators were gone, swept back to their distant homes by hurricane warnings. Linc was not among the few people left beyond the rope. Fear shot coldly through her. She searched with a growing sense of panic. Surely he hadn't left without saying good-bye?

When she heard her own thoughts, the extent of her own uncertainty and vulnerability shocked her. In the last four days Linc had watched her work, asked her about the details he didn't understand, been civil to Roger and charming to the rest of the people. She had told herself that he was finally coming to understand how little the reality of modeling had to do with the irresponsible, amoral women who had been his mother and stepmother. She had told herself that he was coming to appreciate the amount of talent and training and plain hard work that went into her career. She had allowed herself to hope he was changing his mind, outgrowing the past . . . but her panic when she didn't see him waiting told her how fragile her hopes really were.

Deep inside she was haunted by the knowledge that each moment with him could be the last. He didn't believe she loved him, because beautiful women were too selfish to love anyone. She knew he didn't love her . . . yet. Yet. A universe of possibilities in a single word. Yet. So long as they were together there was always hope that she could make him believe she loved him. When he believed, perhaps then he would finally be able to let go of the past and be able to love her in return. At the very least he would stop hating.

Until then, she would live in fear of losing all that she had given to him.

She hurried into the dressing tent, changed with a disregard for her clothes that would have shocked Roger and ran outside. As she searched the spectators for Linc's tall form, she knew that when she found him—if she found him—she would have to force him to talk to her. The "tomorrow" he kept putting off had finally come.

"Shannon?"

She turned and saw one of the technicians waving at her.

"Linc said he would be in your room if you got through early," called the technician.

Holly flashed him a smile that was startling in its beauty. "Thanks," she said breathlessly. She ran toward the hotel, leaving behind an entirely bemused technician.

Linc was propped on the bed, wearing only a towel wrapped around his hips. His hair was still slightly damp from the shower. Arabian stud books and breeding charts were spread around him. A faint patina of moisture covered his naked chest. The light in the room was dim yet oddly luminous. It was the sourceless, pervasive illumination peculiar to storms. Drapes swirled fitfully at either side of the open balcony doors. Like her, Linc preferred fresh air of almost any temperature to the stale, claustrophobic comfort of hotel air conditioning.

"Thought I'd lost you," she said lightly.

He made a noncommittal sound, wrote another note along the margin of a chart, then looked up. "You're off early."

"We're finished." She stretched. "Five glorious days of vacation, beginning now. Well, four, actually. Today's about gone. Roger said we can stay here if we like, but I said you'd probably want to go home." As he glanced out of the window at the unsettled sky, she added, "Unless the center of the storm comes through, none of the flights will be canceled."

"You're really off?" he asked skeptically, turning back to her. The length of her work hours—the fact that the Royce Reflection was essentially on call twenty-four hours a day, every day—had made Linc very angry at first. Then he had simply ignored the subject, accepting her long hours with outward indifference.

Holly hesitated. "I'm off like you're off at the ranch—until something goes wrong. Or in my case, right." She sighed. "Whenever the ad company finally brings in the perfume campaign Roger wants, I'll have to fly to whatever place they've picked as a suitable backdrop."

"Hasn't Roger heard of studio shots?" asked Linc dryly.

"He loathes them. Says all that control kills the sensual surprise."

Linc grunted and gathered up his papers.

"Don't let me interrupt," said Holly quickly. "I know you must be getting behind in your work."

He stacked the books and papers on the bedside table, then pulled her onto the bed. Off-balance, she fell across his lap. Before she could recover, his mouth was on hers.

"Mmmm. Peppermint." He licked her lips appreciatively.

Holly felt warmth spread throughout her in liquid waves. It would be so easy to let go, to be like clouds gathered against a mountain's hard planes, growing and filling until the world shattered into lightning, and thunder rolled and rain came down, fusing cloud and mountain into a single entity. It would be so easy . . . but if she and Linc didn't talk, one day she would wake up and find that he had gone, taking her love with him and never knowing it.

"Linc," she said, turning away. "We have to talk."

"Later," he murmured, shifting her in his arms so that she couldn't escape.

"Tomorrow?"

"Yes." The tip of his tongue teased the curve of her ear. "Tomorrow."

"You've said that before."

"What's the hurry?" he asked, catching her chin in his hand. "Tomorrow will always be there."

"And we'll always be *here.*"

His fingers tightened on her chin until she couldn't move. "Are you tired of me already?" he asked, his face as neutral as his voice.

For an instant Holly was too shocked to speak. Then she wrapped her arms around him and hugged him fiercely. "I'll never be tired of you, Linc. I love you."

She felt him stiffen in rejection. Fear returned in cold waves. Somehow she had to make him believe that she loved him, because until he believed that, he would never believe that his own love would be safe with a beautiful woman. They needed to talk about that and about many other things, yet the only communication he permitted was the wordless language of sensuality.

Slowly she began taking off her clothes, not stopping until she was as naked as the clouds gathering beyond the windows, clouds looking for mountains to call down their rain.

"I know you don't believe me," she said, her voice soft, urgent. "You think words are nothing, less than breath." She looked down at him, her tawny eyes huge with her need to make him understand. "Listen to my hands, to my body. Let me tell you of my love. Then you'll have to believe me. Please, Linc. Listen . . ."

Surprised by the intensity of her plea, he made no objection when she gently pushed him back down onto the bed. "I don't get to touch you as much as I want, not like this," she murmured, fingers sliding deeply into his hair. "Your hair feels cool, like rough silk between my fingers. There are so many colors in it, chestnut and bronze, molten gold, even black." She leaned over. "Your hair smells good, twilight rain with the heat of the desert welling up from beneath."

She closed her eyes for a moment, feeling his hair slide over the sensitive skin between her fingers. Delicately, then with greater confidence, her fingertips rubbed over his scalp, seeking out and loosening tight muscles. He sighed and closed his eyes, giving himself over to the pleasure of her knowing fingers. She kneaded down toward his neck, then back up to trace the contours of his ears with her fingernails. His breathing shortened.

With a soft laugh, she bent down and nuzzled his ear. "I wondered if you were sensitive there, too," she whispered, her breath another kind of caress. The tip of her tongue probed lightly, searching out and finding every sensitive point, then moving slowly in and out.

"Holly—" he said, his voice already thick, his arms pinning her suddenly against his body.

"You're supposed to listen, Linc," she said, her teeth closing gently on the rim of his ear. "You can't listen if you're touching me."

"I don't know how much of this 'listening' I can take," he said, but his arms loosened, allowing her freedom again.

"I've hardly started," she breathed. "There's so much more I want to tell you." Her teeth moved down, tracing the strong tendons of his neck. Her palms massaged the swell of muscle where neck and shoulders joined. "Your neck, for instance. The muscles fit so perfectly against my palms. It feels . . . complete . . . when my palms curve around you."

His after-shave was so subtle she couldn't smell it until her lips rubbed over his neck. His freshly shaved skin was neither soft nor rough, simply very masculine in its texture. She savored it with an unhurried kiss, then sighed and moved upward to nibble on his chin.

"But I'm getting ahead of myself. I haven't even mentioned your eyes, whiskey with emerald glints, and those eyelashes . . ." She kissed his eyelids, then gently caught his eyelashes between her lips. "Unfair," she breathed. "I've always thought it was unfair for a man to have such eyes. And your mouth." Her fingertip traced his lips. "When I was thirteen I used to dream of what it would feel like to have those teasing, smiling lips kiss me. All those sensual curves and the hint of power beneath. When I was sixteen I found out that my dreams weren't even a shadow of your kiss."

When he started to say something, she took his mouth with her kiss. Her tongue explored his warmth with a thoroughness that he had taught her. She played with the rough surface of his tongue, the smoothness beneath, the hard serrations of his teeth. At last she lifted her head and sighed, letting the heat of her pleasure flow over his lips. "You still taste like sage and rain and lightning."

Blindly, his lips sought hers again. She laughed softly, eluding him, her mouth moving to his shoulder. She put her teeth against the resilient muscle, biting with just enough force to please rather than to hurt. It was another of the many things she had learned from him; it gave her intense pleasure to use what he had taught her, giving back the joy of his teaching.

Her hands smoothed down the line of his arms, cherishing each shift of muscle under his skin, the steel beneath the silk. "Your strength fascinates me," she said, moving her hand in slow motion over his hard chest. "Things that I couldn't budge, you lift casually. Strength to make or break a world . . ." Her eyes darkened, shadow of her own vulnerability. "So different from me," she whispered, a thread of fear in her voice.

Then her fingertips found his flat nipples. She bent down, licked him with teasing strokes. When she caught a nipple between her teeth, his breath came in sharply. "Different, but alike. You're sensitive there, too. Do you feel hot wires all the way to the pit of your stomach when I do this?" she asked, sucking the nipple with lips and tongue.

His hands closed like a vise on her cheeks, forcing her to look at him. In the odd, sourceless light of the room, his eyes glowed like a cat's. He searched her face for long moments, took her mouth in a kiss that was all the more savage for its restraint, and released her.

She slid down his body, catching his chest hair between her fingers and lips. "I like your hair," she said huskily, "but I've already said that, haven't I? Rough and soft at the same time, springy, it tickles almost as nicely as your tongue." Her fingertips traced the contours of his muscled torso to the edge of the towel. "Different again, so powerful . . ," His breathing shortened as her tongue found and teased his navel. "But we're alike here, sensitive."

She followed the line of dark hair from his navel to the edge of the towel. He waited with breath held, then sighed when she left the towel in place. The bed shifted as she moved.

"Ten toes," she said, laughter in her voice. "That's the same for both of us." She nibbled reflectively on his big toe, then giggled when he protested that her tongue between his toes tickled. "But I like your feet," she said. She caught his foot in her hand and rubbed firmly up to his ankle. "Strong, like all of you."

His calf flexed against her kneading fingers, not in protest but in pleasure, as though through her touch he was appreciating his own strength for the first time. She put a knee on either side of his legs and removed the clip that held her hair in place, knowing that he liked the feel of her hair over his bare skin. Shaking her head, she bent over and let the black mass tumble across his legs.

"Alike and different," she sighed. She bit his thigh with measured force, liking the feel of him beneath her tongue. "Your thighs are so hard when you tense them, so powerful even when you're relaxed."

Her hands moved slowly upward, following the clean line of his legs beneath the towel. She separated the folds of cloth until he wore only the black fall of her hair across him. Then she straightened slowly, letting her hair move over him in a long, silky caress.

"Different," she murmured, tracing the outline of him with a fingertip. "Why are all the words to describe our differences either clinical or crude? Why aren't there any to equal your beauty? For you *are* beautiful, Linc. As beautiful to me as I am to you. But there are no words." Her hands moved up the hard curve of his thighs, fitted around him. Slowly, she bent down. "Listen . . ."

With gentle care, she tasted all his textures as he had tasted hers. His breath drew in sharply, caught in his throat, stayed there. She felt excitement radiate through him, felt it in the heat of his flesh and the hard beat of his pulse, felt shudders of desire shake his strength. She heard her name in the long outrush of his breath and grew more bold. The difference of him fascinated and compelled her; she couldn't explore it enough. The soft heat of her mouth touched him in intimate caress. When he cried out wordlessly, telling her of his intense pleasure, a storm of desire broke over her, nearly overwhelming her.

She moved up his body like a cloud over a mountain, covering him with moist warmth. She settled on him with exquisite slowness, sharing the fierce lightning that lanced through him as he was surrounded by her softness. For a timeless instant she held both of them unmoving, suspended in the still center of a passionate storm. Then she blended her body totally with his, matching the urgent rhythms of his need with her own, letting the storm break over both of them until neither knew who was cloud and who was mountain, for both were melded by lightning into an ecstatic whole.

When the last, distant tremor of the storm finally faded between them, Holly stirred against his chest. "I love you," she said softly, seeking his luminous eyes beneath the dense shadows of his lashes. "Do you know that now? I love you."

His eyes shut and his fingers held her chin so brutally that she cried out. When he spoke, his voice was like steel. *"Don't talk about love."*

Fear closed around her, all the more terrible because she had allowed herself to believe that he had accepted

her love in the passionate certainty of their storm.
"That's like telling me not to breathe," she said, her
throat so tight that words could barely squeeze past.
Tears rained silently down her cheeks. "Loving you is
the most—" She gasped as his hand jerked away. She
watched him lift his fingers to his lips, tasting her tears.
"Why won't you believe me?" she asked despairingly.
"If I were just plain Holly, would you let me talk about
love?"

His face changed, showing an instant of grief and
regret that was like knives turning in him. It was no less
painful for her.

"That's it, isn't it?" she whispered. "I'm not Holly to
you anymore. What am I, Linc? What horrible thing
have I done that you won't even let me say the word
love?"

"There's no point in talking about it," he said, closing
his eyes. "You can't change what you are."

"And what is that?"

"A beautiful, selfish woman."

"Selfish . . . ? Because I won't shrug off my responsi-
bilities and break my contract?"

"Yes."

"No," she said, her voice flattened by despair.
"Quitting wouldn't change anything. I'd still be beautiful, Linc. And you'd still hate me for that, wouldn't
you?"

"I . . . don't hate you."

"I don't believe you. Just as you don't believe I love
you." She laughed oddly. "In time, we may both be
right."

Beyond the window thunder muttered among the
clouds and lightning arched invisibly. The drapes belled
inward, twisting sinuously in the wind. Holly shivered,
but it wasn't the tropic storm that chilled her.

"Does turning on every man in sight matter that
much to you?" asked Linc roughly. "Isn't what we just
had enough to satisfy you?"

"I don't give a damn about turning on any man but you." Holly's voice was soft and absolutely certain. Even Linc had to admit to the truth in her words.

"Then quit modeling."

"And prove how selfish I am." Again her voice was soft, certain.

"What is that supposed to mean?"

"Selfish people make others pay for their pleasures. Being with you is the greatest pleasure I've ever known. Replacing me would cost Roger a year of advertising time and millions of dollars. Why should he be the one to pay for my pleasure?"

Linc's face went cold. "That's a lovely way of twisting words to suit your purposes. But I shouldn't complain if Roger gets the benefit of your talents. He's certainly given you—and me—the benefit of his."

"I don't understand," said Holly. She froze, suddenly sure that she didn't want to understand Linc's meaning. But it was too late. He was already talking, breaking apart her world.

"It's quite simple," he said. His voice was almost indifferent, but his eyes were not. "In the five days I wasn't with you, Roger taught you more about making love than most women learn in a lifetime. I'm not complaining. You've stayed in my bed while I'm here. What more can I ask of a beautiful woman?"

"Don't do this to me," she whispered, retreating from him until his hands caught her, held her with uncaring strength. She felt herself breaking. "Let me go."

His eyebrow lifted. "Why? Is Roger finally getting impatient?"

"I've never touched Roger. He's never touched me." Her voice was thin, patient, as distant as an echo. He could break her world, but not her. *Not her.* She would not break, not even for him. "If I've pleased you in bed, congratulate yourself. You're one hell of a teacher."

She watched disbelief cross his face and felt the same knives of regret and rage turning in her that she had sensed earlier in him. "I came to you as a virgin, something you didn't believe until too late. I can hardly come to you each time as a virgin, and you won't believe in my love." Her laugh sounded like a sob. "You told me to trust you, Linc. And I did. Twice. You have yet to trust me, really trust me, once."

"Holly—" No words followed, nothing but an agonizing silence.

"Tell me that you trust me," she said coaxingly. "Tell me that you love me." She watched his eyes, his lips, the shadows of emotion tightening his face, and she heard all her fears confirmed in his silence. "Never mind, Linc," she said finally, her voice terribly controlled, almost gentle. "It doesn't matter anymore."

"Holly, don't do this," he said, echoing her earlier plea.

"Do what? Tell the truth? Somewhere deep in your mind you're certain that loving a beautiful woman means destroying yourself. Given that, I don't blame you for not loving me. You're strong. You want to survive. But I do blame you for taking revenge on me for something I never did, never would do, never *could* do to you."

She paused, listening to the thunder outside as though it were another aspect of their conversation. She watched him, the last flicker of hope lambent in her eyes, waiting for him to speak.

"It isn't revenge," he said finally. "I don't blame you for what my mother and stepmother did."

"You don't trust me, so you can't love me. It might as well be revenge. I thought that, in time, I could change your feelings." She laughed sadly. "I was very young, wasn't I? I didn't realize that I might learn to hate before you learned to love. But I won't stay around that long, because hating you would destroy me. There would be nothing left."

Thunder curled through the room, sound without meaning.

She looked at him with eyes that no longer asked to be loved. "I thought I could teach you about love. But you were the teacher, Linc. You taught me about hate."

"No," he said, his voice hoarse with pain. His hands rubbed her chill flesh, trying to bring back warmth. "I don't hate you. I never meant to hurt you. No," he said, as she moved to get off the bed. "Let me hold you."

She slid beyond his reach. "You can't give comfort to me any more than I can erase the past for you." She looked at him, feeling tears burn inside her, knowing she would not cry. Tears were born of hope, and she had none left. "Just chalk it up to a case of mistaken identity. You thought I was your sweet Holly, and I thought you were the Linc I had always loved. We were both wrong . . ."

She closed her eyes and turned away. "Good-bye, Linc."

She walked to the window and watched the sky seethe with unshed rain. She did not turn around until she heard the door close behind the man she loved.

12

~oooooooooo~

Holly drove the Jeep with the same restrained savagery that had characterized her movements during the last hundred days. Behind her a caravan of four-wheel-drive vehicles raised clouds of grit out of the dry, rutted road. The time of summer thunder was over. It was as though the rains of June had been only a dream. The fragrant bloom of chaparral and flowers had come and gone as quickly as a blush. All that remained was the smell of heat and dust and drought. The land was empty again, waiting in September's burning silence for the enduring renewal of winter rains.

She looked up to the mountains just once. and then couldn't look again. Barren, desolate, compelling in their power, the silent mountains spoke eloquently of Linc. She wouldn't answer. She wouldn't even call his name in the quiet of her own mind.

Behind her the caravan dropped back farther with each minute. She neither noticed nor cared. She had argued with Roger about returning to Hidden Springs. There was no need—the Royce Is Romance campaign was already wrapped up. The Desert Designs campaign didn't require a Hidden Springs location. Any dry place would do. Why not Egypt—history and pyramids and enigmas baking under the sun? But Roger had insisted on Hidden Springs. She had fought against it up to the point of breaking her contract. That she did not want to do. Her work was all she had left. And Roger had known it. He had won.

It was all he had won, though. When he had realized that Linc was no longer part of her life, Roger had offered to fill the emptiness he saw. She had refused him with a polite, cool finality that was totally unlike her earlier unease at his proposals. When he persisted, she told him that if the subject ever came up again, she would leave and never look back—she had walked away from more in order to survive. After a week of uncomfortable silence, Roger had resumed treating her with witty camaraderie.

The sands of Antelope Wash spun off the Jeep's tires in dry fountains. Grit showered over the windshield, coating everything. She didn't notice. If she had, she wouldn't have slowed the churning wheels by even a bit. She pushed the Jeep out to the edge of its performance and held it there with the same ruthless concentration she had used lately when she worked, retreating to a place where there was—if not peace—at least momentary release from memory.

Linc had called her a week after Cabo San Lucas. She had asked if he had anything new to say to her, and as she asked, hope was a terrible ache in her. He had spoken of his hunger and need . . . and she had hung up because she couldn't bear to hear her own agony in his voice. Hunger wasn't enough. If it were, she would never have left him.

She hadn't taken any more of his calls. The brief return of hope had hurt too much, reminding her of what it had been like to feel a dream come true, to love him, to be alive . . .

In time, he had stopped calling.

The Jeep spurted up over the last ridge separating her from Hidden Springs. When she saw the three horses and riders waiting at her former campsite, she abruptly sent the Jeep into a controlled skid, stopping in a shower of stones and dirt. She fought her impulse to hurtle the Jeep back the same way she had come. She sat unmoving behind the wheel, watching Linc not a hundred feet away.

He turned and looked at her, consuming her in a single glance. She felt the relentless heat of the sun pushing her down, flattening her, and the world falling away beneath her. There was nothing supporting her but his intense regard, and soon he would look away, leaving her to fall endlessly.

She closed her eyes and hung on to the steering wheel. She had not known until this instant how close to the edge of her world she had been living, how easy it would be to fall off. She couldn't let him do this to her.

"Holly?"

It was Beth's voice, not Linc's. Holly gathered what was left of herself and opened her eyes. Beth was walking toward her, a big yellow dog tangling in her feet. Holly opened the door and forced herself to get out, ruffle Freedom's ears when he bounded up to greet her, and smile at the approaching girl. It wasn't Beth's fault that Holly loved the wrong man.

"Hello, Beth," said Holly, her voice rich with many emotions. She opened her arms and hugged the girl, saying to her what she couldn't say to Linc. "I've missed you."

Beth's voice caught in a sob. She hung onto Holly for long moments before she could speak. "Why—" Then, quickly, "No, I promised myself I wouldn't ask. How are you, Holly? You look different. Like Linc. Older."

Holly didn't answer. Instead, she took off the western hat that all but concealed the girl's face. Holly caught her breath. Beth was exquisite. Her hair fell around her shoulders in a radiant tide, framing her face in smoldering honey curls. She wore just enough makeup to bring out the turquoise brilliance of her eyes. Beneath a transparent gloss, her lips were vulnerable, inviting, innocent.

"You've grown into your beauty," said Holly. "How does Linc feel about—?" She stopped abruptly. Linc's reaction was none of her business. "You look happy, Beth. I'm glad."

"Linc doesn't mind that I'm beautiful. Not anymore. Four weeks after he came back from Cabo San Lucas, he took me to Palm Springs. New clothes, new hairstyle, new makeup, everything I ever wanted except you for my sister." Beth blinked back tears. "Linc wants me to be whatever I can be, Holly. He loves me."

Holly felt the world falling away again. "I'm happy for you," she whispered, surprised that she could speak past the numbness gripping her.

"Come back to the ranch with me," said Beth, words tumbling over each other in her rush to speak before Holly stopped her. "Linc loves you, I know he does. He hasn't seen Cyn or any other woman. All he's done is work like there's no tomorrow. He's awful to everyone except me. He's been so gentle with me that sometimes I just want to cry. Please come back. He loves—"

"No." Holly heard the harshness of her voice. Much more gently she said, "No, Beth. But thank you. Now that you and Linc understand each other, maybe he'll let you come with me, instead. I'm going to Rio soon. Or is it Santiago . . . ?" She shrugged. "I forget which. Would you like to go?"

Excitement made Beth look younger, then excitement faded. "I don't know if Linc would let me miss school. I'm only here today because I threatened awful things if I didn't get the chance to see you."

Holly's smile was wistful. She hadn't realized quite how lonely she had been until she thought of taking Beth with her, having someone to share her world with.

"Maybe during Thanksgiving or Christmas vacation . . . no, those are family times. Linc will need you then." She forced a convincing professional smile onto her face; she had become very good at that in the last few months. "Don't look so sad. There's always next summer."

"It's not that. It's just—who will you spend those family times with?" she blurted.

Wishing that Beth were old enough not to ask such questions, Holly replaced Beth's hat with a firm tug. "Who's the handsome man with you?"

"You mean Linc?" asked Beth, confused.

"No."

"Oh. Jack. I don't think of him as a man. Not like Linc, anyway."

Holly felt her smile slipping. She knew better than Beth ever would how few men like Linc there were in the world.

"Come on," said Beth. "I want to introduce you."

Holly wished she hadn't driven so fast to the springs. If the others were here, she would have had an excuse to avoid Linc. As it was, she could run like a scared child or she could walk over there and pretend there was no reason not to talk to him.

"Holly?"

"Coming," she said tightly.

Beth took her hand and led her over to Jack. He saw them coming and dismounted. Linc did not. Holly felt a bittersweet relief that she wouldn't have to stand close to him. She smiled and shook Jack's hand, said polite, meaningless words and wished she had turned and run like the scared child she was. She couldn't look at Linc, too close, so far away. The pressure of his presence was like the sun, burning her skin, melting her bones, making her dizzy for lack of cool air to breathe.

"Aren't you even going to say hello to Linc?" asked Beth.

Holly turned and glanced at him with unfocused eyes, looking without seeing. "Hello, Linc."

There was a small silence. Then, "I've missed you, *niña.*"

The world dipped beneath her, time peeling away until she was nine again, standing on hot sand looking up at Linc, knowing somewhere deep inside herself that she would love this man and no other. But he wasn't seventeen anymore, and she wasn't nine.

She stared up at him as though she had never seen him before. He was more powerful than she had remembered. When his horse shifted restlessly, Linc's shoulders blocked out the sun. Beneath the thick screen of lashes, his eyes searched hers, looking for something they both had lost. His face was harder, thinner, drawn with the inner tension that radiated from him. Like a caged lion, he waited for . . . what?

The saddle creaked as Linc shifted his weight. She realized she had been staring up at him for a long time. Beth and Jack had retreated somewhere, leaving her to face the ruins of her dream with no support, no shield, no place to hide. She was shocked at the pain she felt, appalled that she could still feel at all. Then she knew with terrible finality that her capacity to be hurt by Linc was as great as her love for him. There was no end to her vulnerability. If he touched her, she would be destroyed. She didn't have the strength to leave him again.

He had called her *niña.*

In the distance she heard the sounds of vehicles laboring over the last ridge to Hidden Springs. She didn't know she had turned and fled toward the caravan until she felt herself gasping for air beneath the hammerblows of the sun. She stopped abruptly, lungs aching as she fought for breath. The air was as harsh and dry as stone.

The first Jeep came over the hill. When he saw Holly Roger signaled the driver to stop.

"What are you doing here? Did your Jeep break down?"

"No." She climbed into the back seat, ignoring Roger's offer of his lap. "Just thought I'd see what was taking you so long."

Roger stared at her, then at the horse approaching the Jeep, and the rider. "Did he—"

"No," she interrupted curtly.

Roger said nothing more. He had learned that when she took that tone of voice, there was no point in pursuing the subject.

"Hello, Roger," said Linc, reining in his horse next to the idling Jeep.

Holly felt chills chase themselves over her arms. Just the sound of Linc's voice unnerved her. She refused to look higher than the stirrup that brushed against her side of the vehicle. Yet she couldn't help but see his sinuous power as he controlled the restless horse. She remembered what it had felt like to knead his muscular leg, to test its resilience with teeth and tongue, to savor his compelling differences. With a small sound she closed her eyes and looked at nothing at all.

"Hello, Linc. Beautiful animal you're riding. I should have taken Shannon's suggestion and arranged to use your horses for some shots."

"Holly suggested that?" asked Linc, more intensity in his voice than such a simple question would require.

"Yes, when she first suggested using Hidden Springs."

"But not lately?" asked Linc, intensity fading.

"No," said Roger bluntly. "In fact, she nearly broke her contract rather than come back this time."

Silently, Holly wished that Roger would shut up.

"But she came," continued Roger relentlessly. "She's a real pro."

"Yes," said Linc in a neutral voice. "I know that her work means more to her than . . . anything."

Holly caught herself shaking her head in a despairing negative. She stopped, but not before Linc and Roger saw.

"Wrong," said Roger, his voice very clipped. "She told me that if I didn't behave, I could take my contract and paper the loo with it." He smiled thinly. "Yes, I thought that would please you. So I dragged her back to you, though I doubt that you deserve her. Now if you'll kindly wave your magic wand and put the light and laughter back in Shannon, I'll—"

"That's enough, Roger," said Holly, her voice brittle, balanced on the thin edge of breaking. "Just. Shut. Up."

Roger said something very inelegant beneath his breath, but offered no more comments. Holly felt Linc study her, but refused to look at him. Coming back to Hidden Springs had been a mistake. She hadn't realized how bad a mistake until now.

"Did Holly warn you about snakes?" asked Linc as though nothing had happened.

"Snakes?" Roger turned and looked at Holly.

Holly shrugged. "I warned the technicians. They'll be the ones banging about. They should scare off any snakes that might be around."

"Might?" asked Linc sardonically. "Holly, you know damn well there are always snakes around the springs."

She shrugged again. "I won't be the first one in the underbrush, so there's no problem."

Linc turned to Roger. "If Holly gets nailed by a rattler, she's dead."

"The hell you say! I didn't know the beggars were that lethal," said Roger, staring at Linc's hard face.

"They aren't, unless a big one gets you on the

neck—or you're violently allergic to venom, like Holly. Then you are dead." He spaced the last words carefully, so there could be no mistaking his meaning.

Roger tapped the driver's arm. "Turn around."

"Don't be ridiculous," snapped Holly. "I stand a better chance of getting killed in a car crash."

"The way you drove in here," said Linc under his breath, "I believe it."

Roger looked doubtful. "You're sure, Shannon?"

"Yes." Her voice, like her mouth, was inflexible.

He hesitated, then sighed. "Right. Let's get on with it, then."

"Not yet." Linc's blunt command startled Holly. She looked up—and froze, held by the hazel certainty in his eyes. "After you're finished working, *niña*, we'll talk."

"No," said Holly too quickly. "We don't have anything new to say to each other."

But Linc had spun his horse and cantered away before the first word was out of her mouth.

Holly was perched on a pile of boulders that was as big as a house. She leaned against one particularly massive stone, hands spread on the hot surface, fingernails gleaming with the color of a desert sunset. A matching color fired her lips. It was the cosmetics, not the clothes, that were being emphasized in this series of shots.

"Over your right shoulder this time," directed Jerry.

She turned her head with a sinuous motion that made her hair fly. She challenged the camera with her tawny eyes, her unsmiling lips, the perfect black curves of her eyebrows. "Catch Me if You Can" was the theme of the Desert Designs campaign, and she was quintessentially the elusive woman poised on the brink of flight.

"Fantastic! Again. Now right. Again. Again. Again."

She responded to Jerry's commands with reflex precision that always managed to look spontaneous, intimate. That, too, was her trademark—the flexible beauty that made photographers fight for the opportunity to work with her.

"Okay. Break for reload." Jerry looked up at her, perched precariously above him on a jumble of boulders. "Not enough time to climb down, lovey, unless you need some more sunscreen goo."

She shrugged. "I'm all right."

She looked beyond Jerry, past the technicians and their lights and reflectors, the makeup man and hairstylist, the sultan's tent where she changed from one desert-inspired outfit to another. The slanting light of late afternoon made even the smallest pebble leap out of its background and turned granite boulders into soft textures of gold. Beyond the hubbub of the set, the desert animals were beginning to move out into the coolness, released from the sun's seamless prison.

Linc was off to the left, well out of the way of the technicians setting up more reflectors. He sat on his dark horse, relaxed and powerful in his waiting, as patient as the desert itself. Jack was close to Linc, standing in the stirrups, peering behind the boulders where Holly was. Beth's horse stood near a large clump of brush, but she was not in the saddle.

Behind Holly's pile of boulders, Freedom suddenly started barking. Just as the barks reached a frantic pitch, Beth's scream ripped through the afternoon silence. Instantly Holly leaped from boulder to boulder, heading for Beth, heedless of the height and the danger of falling. Out of the corner of her eye she saw both men spur their horses into a dead run. But they had a long way to go and Beth was screaming, her voice raw with terror.

As Holly scrambled over the top of the boulder pile, she saw what Linc and Jack had seen—Beth frozen in fear, staring down at the ground where Freedom barked and made passes at a snake coiled in the sand. The snake was effectively trapped between the screaming girl and the snapping, snarling dog. It divided its reptilian attention between the two threats.

Beth stopped screaming as suddenly as she had begun. Holly started running as she saw the girl sway forward alarmingly, on the verge of fainting. If Beth fainted, she would fall on top of the snake. Then it would strike mindlessly, again and again, for that was the nature of a frightened snake. It could hardly miss Beth's face and her neck, the points of greatest vulnerability.

Freedom barked and started toward the snake. Holly skidded to a stop, hoping that the dog would keep the snake's attention off the pale, terrified girl.

"It's all right, Beth," said Holly in a reassuring voice, easing forward, measuring the distance between girl and snake. Not enough. Any sudden movement could trigger the snake's strike. She couldn't risk yanking Beth out of danger. She would have to get between Beth and the rattler. That way Beth wouldn't fall onto the snake if she fainted.

Beth moaned and swayed, drawing the snake's black-eyed attention. Seeing an opening, Freedom rushed in, then leaped back as the snake struck at him. Holly slid between Beth and the snake and caught the girl as her knees gave way. She hadn't quite fainted, but she was no longer able to stand. Holly braced herself and supported Beth, trying to hold both of them absolutely motionless.

And then Holly realized what she had done. She was standing in silk shorts and sandals less than three feet away from a coiled, buzzing rattler. She knew a snake couldn't strike more than its own length, but she had no way of knowing how long the rattler was. She stared sideways at the snake in blank fascination, trying to guess its length from the thickness of its coils.

Beth gave an odd moan. Holly murmured reassurances through stiff lips and held Beth more tightly, afraid that any movement would take the snake's attention off the snarling, leaping dog.

Out of the corner of her eye she saw Linc's Arabian race by and come to a rearing, plunging stop well behind Freedom. A reflector flashed vividly in the sun as Linc leaped off, holding the flexible steel panel in one hand. He called off the dog in a voice that compelled obedience. Whining, reluctant, Freedom came to heel.

Linc moved toward the snake with the odd, gliding motion of a stalking animal. The reflector burned gold in his hand. His eyes were intent, focused on the deadly, poised head of the rattlesnake. It watched his approach with unblinking attention, quivering along its thick length, making a sound like pine needles shaken in a paper bag.

Slowly, Linc raised the reflector above his head, holding the metal securely in one gloved hand. There was no warning. He simply surged forward and brought the reflector down in the same fast, deadly motion. The steel edge sliced through the snake and didn't stop until it grated on rock buried six inches beneath the sand.

Holly closed her eyes, shutting out the reflexive writhings of the dead snake. She heard Beth's choked cry as Jack lifted her out of Holly's arms. She heard Jack speaking broken words of fear and relief, wrapping Beth in protective strength. Then they stood and held onto each other with silent intensity.

Holly watched them and felt an instant of piercing envy. Her life was like the time before dawn, neither stars nor sunrise to grace the hollow arch of the sky, only a vast emptiness waiting to be filled.

Hands closed cruelly around her arms, spinning her around, shaking her.

"That's the most stupid stunt I've ever seen anyone pull!" shouted Linc. "Do you think you can't die? What the hell were you trying to prove?"

She stared at him. His face was like the stone she had touched earlier, harsh and unyielding. His eyes were narrowed, blazing with rage, his lips thinned over his teeth as he yelled at her. Behind her she heard Jack's low words of comfort to Beth. Laughter hurt her, clawing to be free, a laughter as feral as his eyes. She clenched her teeth against it.

"Beth was going to faint," she said. Her voice belonged to someone else, thin and calm, empty. "She was swaying forward. . . . The snake . . ." She saw his expression change as he realized the kind of danger Beth had been in. "Good," she said distinctly. "I'm glad you can care . . . about somebody."

Behind her came the sound of Beth's tears and Jack's soft words of comfort. Holly wondered what it would be like to cry again, to have someone hold her, care about her, taste her tears and make them his own. Linc had done that for her the night her parents had died. He had held her world together with his strength and his love. She had drawn on that night for six years, her secret well of dreams and courage. She had gone alone into an intensely competitive career in a world far removed from her childhood, and she had conquered it. She had come back to share her world with him, the world he had given her the strength to build; but he hadn't wanted either her world or her. And now her strength was running out of her like water, draining color and warmth, leaving behind nothing at all.

She heard her voice at a great distance and realized

she had been thinking aloud. But it no longer mattered. She had lost her balance and fallen off the edge of the world, spinning into the darkness below.

She woke up slowly, all the colors of sunset blazing and rippling overhead. She heard men's voices arguing, Roger and Linc, and she pulled a flame-colored satin sheet over her head. She couldn't face Linc, not yet. She couldn't even face herself. With a long sigh, she let her exhausted body sink into sleep.

When she woke again, she wondered where she was. She saw the brilliant colors of the sultan's canopy overhead and remembered using it as a backdrop for Desert Designs. But she was wearing the wrong costume now, shorts rather than harem pants, and why was one of the satin tent dividers covering her? Memory returned. She realized that she had fainted for the first time in her life. Afterward, she vaguely remembered hearing an argument between Linc and Roger, cars starting, leaving. And then she had slept.

Linc.

Even as she thought his name, she knew he was nearby, alone with her in the desert. She sensed him watching her, a presence as powerful as the mountains, and as unyielding. Fingertips stroked her face. She flinched away, not able to endure being hurt again, wishing suddenly that she had not awakened at all. The quiet surrounding the canopy was absolute.

The warmth of his body flowed along her side as he lay next to her. Protest rippled through her, a spasm of stiffness that passed quickly because she hadn't the strength to sustain it. She felt the thick weight of her hair lifted off her neck, only to be replaced by his lips burning against her skin in a caress that was all the more consuming for its gentleness.

"No. Don't."

He heard the pleading in her voice, and the fear beneath it. "Why?"

"Nothing's changed," she said, then laughed abruptly. "Bad to worse. That's a change, isn't it?"

"Everything has changed, *niña*. I love you."

She put her hand against her mouth and bit into her own skin to keep from crying out in protest. Too late . . . too late. She couldn't believe him, couldn't allow herself to believe him, because if she was wrong, if she let herself hope and love and live again only to lose him . . . "No."

"Look at me," he said gently.

She closed her eyes.

He kissed her eyelids, then carefully took her hand away from her mouth and kissed the livid marks her teeth had left on her skin. He talked softly, as though to himself. "I've loved Holly from the first time I saw her staring up at me on the trail with her heart in her eyes. But I was seventeen and she was only nine. I watched her grow up until one night she ran out of my parents' house and threw herself into my arms. I wanted to kill my parents for frightening her. I took her home, kissed her, kissed her again and again, wanting her . . ."

She tried to say something, to make him stop retelling her dream in his words, but he kept talking in a voice that was husky with desire and regret and an emotion she was afraid to name, much less believe.

"The next night I held her again, but differently. Her parents were dying, and she wept in my arms and I learned that shared grief was as binding as shared desire. She let me hold her, cry with her, love her. And then she was gone."

He paused, remembering, and his eyes were dark. "I never wanted a woman as much as I wanted Holly, until six years later in Palm Springs, when a cat-eyed, black-haired model held out her arms to me and promised me . . . everything."

She moved restlessly, wanting to stop him, not wanting to live through it all with him again, knowing how it would end. Gentle, relentless, his voice continued over her unspoken objections.

"Suddenly I understood what had happened to my father. I no longer hated him, but I knew I would hate myself if I gave in. I didn't see Holly beneath Shannon's fire. I didn't realize that I wanted Shannon *because* she was Holly. All I saw was a woman beautiful enough to destroy a man's soul. I lashed out, trying to protect myself from the kind of hunger I thought I'd never feel again.

"I couldn't sleep. I saddled the first horse in the barn and set out on the roughest trail I could find. It was a wild night and a damn fool thing to do. But"—his lips brushed her hand—"people who love sometimes do foolish things, like stand in front of rattlesnakes. Thank you, my love. For Beth. I had already figured out that you weren't the selfish woman of my nightmares, but I didn't know just how unselfish you were."

His fingers tightened on hers, radiating warmth through her cold body. She didn't notice that she was holding on as tightly as he was. She was watching him, her eyes tawny in the dying light.

"I had better luck than I deserved that night," said Linc softly, his eyes focused on the past. He might have been talking to himself, but for his long fingers stroking hers, sensing the gradual return of warmth to her skin. "I woke up next to the woman I loved and thought I'd lost. She fitted against me so perfectly, melting in my hands . . ." His voice caught and for a moment there was only the sound of the wind teasing the brilliant canopy.

"Then I found out that Holly was Shannon. I felt betrayed. Afraid. Caught like my father. A fool. I took the only revenge I could and proved what an utter fool I really was. I'll never forgive myself for that, Holly."

She said nothing, only laced her fingers more deeply with his, watching him, something close to hope in her eyes.

"Yet you forgave me," he whispered. "You came to me like a cloud to a mountain, sinking into me like rain, giving life to me. But you were Shannon, too, and I was afraid. Each time we made love you sank more deeply into me. And then you said good-bye because I could not say the simple truth: I love you."

He looked at her. "I don't want you to give up anything for me, certainly not part of yourself. I want you to be everything you can be. I want to add to your life, not subtract from it. I'll travel with you when I can, stay home when I must. Just let me be part of you again. I love you so much. . . ."

His voice caught and his eyes searched hers. "Tell me I'm not too late," he whispered. "Tell me that living without me is like dying every day. Tell me that you'll marry me."

She put her fingers on his lips to stop his words, unable to bear his pain any longer because it was too like her own.

"I love you, Linc."

She felt him tremble beneath her hand, felt the heat of his breath expelled in a long rush. His arms started to draw her in, then stopped. She knew he was remembering the moment when she had awakened and flinched at his touch. She drew his mouth down to hers, breathing her warmth into him.

Slowly their bodies flowed together, healing each other with a touch and a sigh, melting into each other until neither could say whose lips were kissed, whose tears were tasted, who spoke first of the life they would share, children and laughter, dreams as strong as the people who dreamed them . . .

And then there was only silence and need, cloud and mountain, the season of rain and life renewing.

Silhouette Desire
15-Day Trial Offer

A new romance series
that explores
contemporary relationships
in exciting detail

Six Silhouette Desire romances, free for 15 days!
We'll send you six new Silhouette Desire romances
to look over for 15 days, absolutely free! If you decide
not to keep the books, return them and owe nothing.

Six books a month, free home delivery. If you like
Silhouette Desire romances as much as we think you
will, keep them and return your payment with the
invoice. Then we will send you six new books every
month to preview, just as soon as they are published.
You pay only for the books you decide to keep, and
you never pay postage and handling.

YOU'LL BE SWEPT AWAY
WITH SILHOUETTE DESIRE

$1.75 each

1 ☐ CORPORATE AFFAIR
James

2 ☐ LOVE'S SILVER WEB
Monet

3 ☐ WISE FOLLY
Clay

4 ☐ KISS AND TELL
Carey

5 ☐ WHEN LAST WE LOVED
Baker

6 ☐ A FRENCHMAN'S KISS
Mallory

7 ☐ NOT EVEN FOR LOVE
St. Claire

8 ☐ MAKE NO PROMISES
Dee

9 ☐ MOMENT IN TIME
Simms

10 ☐ WHENEVER I LOVE YOU
Smith

$1.95 each

11 ☐ VELVET TOUCH
James

12 ☐ THE COWBOY AND THE
LADY   Palmer

13 ☐ COME BACK, MY LOVE
Wallace

14 ☐ BLANKET OF STARS
Valley

15 ☐ SWEET BONDAGE
Vernon

16 ☐ DREAM COME TRUE
Major

17 ☐ OF PASSION BORN
Simms

18 ☐ SECOND HARVEST
Ross

19 ☐ LOVER IN PURSUIT
James

20 ☐ KING OF DIAMONDS
Allison

21 ☐ LOVE INTHE CHINA SEA
Baker

22 ☐ BITTERSWEET IN BERN
Durant

23 ☐ CONSTANT STRANGER
Sunshine

24 ☐ SHARED MOMENTS
Baxter

25 ☐ RENAISSANCE MAN
James

26 ☐ SEPTEMBER MORNING
Palmer

27 ☐ ON WINGS OF NIGHT
Conrad

28 ☐ PASSIONATE JOURNEY
Lovan

29 ☐ ENCHANTED DESERT
Michelle

30 ☐ PAST FORGETTING
Lind

31 ☐ RECKLESS PASSION
James

32 ☐ YESTERDAY'S DREAMS
Clay

38 ☐ SWEET SERENITY
Douglass

39 ☐ SHADOW OF BETRAYAL
Monet

40 ☐ GENTLE CONQUEST
Mallory

41 ☐ SEDUCTION BY DESIGN
St. Claire

42 ☐ ASK ME NO SECRETS
Stewart

43 ☐ A WILD, SWEET MAGIC
Simms

44 ☐ HEART OVER MIND West

45 ☐ EXPERIMENT IN LOVE Clay

46 ☐ HER GOLDEN EYES Chance

47 ☐ SILVER PROMISES Michelle

48 ☐ DREAM OF THE WEST
Powers

49 ☐ AFFAIR OF HONOR James

Silhouette Desire

SILHOUETTE DESIRE, Department SD/6
1230 Avenue of the Americas
New York, NY 10020

Please send me the books I have checked above. I am enclosing $_____
(please add 50¢ to cover postage and handling. NYS and NYC residents please add
appropriate sales tax.) Send check or money order—no cash or C.O.D.'s please.
Allow six weeks for delivery.

NAME _____

ADDRESS _____

CITY _____ STATE/ZIP _____

Enjoy your own special time with Silhouette Romances.

Send for 6 books today– one is yours <u>free</u>!

Silhouette Romances take you into a special world of thrilling drama, tender passion, and romantic love. These are enthralling stories from your favorite romance authors—tales of fascinating men and women, set in exotic locations all over the world.

Convenient free home delivery. We'll send you six exciting Silhouette Romances to look over for 15 days. If you enjoy them as much as we think you will, pay the invoice enclosed with your trial shipment. **One book is yours free to keep.** Silhouette Romances are delivered right to your door with never a charge for postage or handling. There's no minimum number of books to buy, and you may cancel at any time.

Silhouette Romances

READERS' COMMENTS ON SILHOUETTE DESIRES

"Thank you for Silhouette Desires. They are the best thing that has happened to the bookshelves in a long time."
—V.W.*, Knoxville, TN

"Silhouette Desires—wonderful, fantastic—the best romance around."
—H.T.*, Margate, N.J.

"As a writer as well as a reader of romantic fiction, I found DESIREs most refreshingly realistic—and definitely as magical as the love captured on their pages."
—C.M.*, Silver Lake, N.Y.

*names available on request